PLAYING THE
Field

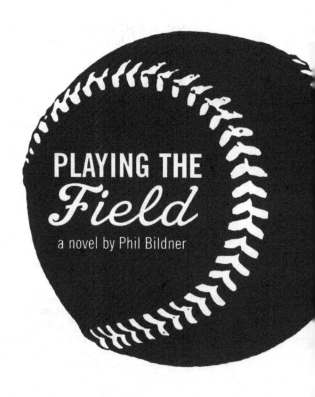

PLAYING THE
Field

a novel by Phil Bildner

Simon & Schuster Books for Young Readers

New York   London   Toronto   Sydney

SIMON & SCHUSTER BOOKS FOR YOUNG READERS
An imprint of Simon & Schuster Children's Publishing Division
1230 Avenue of the Americas, New York, New York 10020

This book is a work of fiction. Any references to historical events, real people, or real locales are used fictitiously. Other names, characters, places, and incidents are products of the author's imagination, and any resemblance to actual events or locales or persons, living or dead, is entirely coincidental.

SIMON & SCHUSTER BOOKS FOR YOUNG READERS is a trademark of Simon & Schuster, Inc.
Book design by Lucy Ruth Cummins
The text for this book is set in Electra LH.
Manufactured in the United States of America
2 4 6 8 10 9 7 5 3 1
Library of Congress Cataloging-in-Publication Data
Bildner, Phil.
Playing the field / Phil Bildner—1st ed.
p. cm.
Summary: When seventeen-year-old Darcy Miller pretends to be a lesbian in order to play on the baseball team, she must learn to battle discrimination on every playing field.
ISBN-13: 978-1-4814-2172-0
ISBN-10: 1-4169-0284-8 (hardcover)
[1. Sex role—Fiction. 2. Homosexuality—Fiction. 3. Baseball—Fiction. 4. High schools—Fiction. 5. Schools—Fiction.] I. Title.
PZ7.B4923Pl 2006
[Fic]—dc22 2004024396

FIRST EDITION

*To Corey, Jennifer, and Kevin—the dreamers
in my life who never stop believing*

Acknowledgments

Phil would like to thank and acknowledge . . .

Emily Thomas, my wonderful editor, for believing in Darcy

*Ed Robertson and the Barenaked Ladies for their irreverent inspiration,
and for helping to provide a soundtrack to my life*

*The Gay-Straight Alliance Network (www.gsanetwork.org)
and the Gay, Lesbian, Straight Education Network (www.glsen.org).
Much of the data contained in* Playing the Field *comes from their National
School Climate Survey.*

1

"Let's . . . let's try to settle down here. Don't out—"

"Don't talk to me like I'm a golden retriever!" Nathalie roared.

I chomped on my tongue.

I couldn't remember the last time I had seen my mom this worked up about anything. We were in my principal's office, and Nathalie had one hand pressing down so firmly on his desk that, I swear, she was going to leave a permanent impression, and her other hand was flailing about like a conductor's in front of an orchestra.

As for me? I wasn't saying word one. Zero. *Nada.* I knew better than to disobey Nathalie's direct orders.

"When we're in that office, Darcy," she had said on the ride over, "I'm doing the talking. You're not my tag-team partner, you're not my copilot, and you're certainly not sitting second chair. Do I make myself clear?"

So as Mom and Principal Basset dueled it out, I sat silently, like the dutiful daughter I can be when I want to be.

"I'll go straight to the school board with this." Mom wagged her baton-finger. "You know I will."

"I think we need to calm down and discuss this like adults," Principal Basset replied shakily.

I cringed. He had told her to *calm down*. One thing you never say to Nathalie Miller is "Calm down." That'll shift her into bitch mode in a heartbeat.

You see, Nathalie has a reputation for being, well, high strung. She's one of those staunch believers in standing up for what she feels is right—though I sometimes question her Malcolm X, by-any-means-necessary strategies. Nathalie defends her "spirited" approach by citing her successes in the workplace. She's a vice president at an assertiveness training, personal coach, and cheerleader firm. It's one of those supposedly hip companies where everyone's a vice president of something. To her credit, her straightforward, pull-no-punches style has gotten her some seriously eye-popping and jaw-dropping fringe benefits, including a corner office, a generous salary, an impressive expense account, a family health-club membership, two laptops, a cell phone, four weeks' vacation, and a comprehensive dental plan. So who am I to question when she stretches her tactics and theatrics to venues outside her place of employment?

Mom does recognize—thank god—that her outbursts need to be controlled. She goes to therapy thrice a week, and her therapist, Dr. Jane St. Claire, is a lifesaver. From time to time, I'll even call the good doctor and, on behalf of all those who come into contact with Nathalie, express my sincerest gratitude for the life assistance she started prescribing for my mom way back when I was in elementary school. I'm telling you, without all those little multicolored magic pills, a coronary would have killed her and orphaned me years ago.

Nathalie sat back down, looked over at me, and took several *longdeeplongdeeplongdeep* breaths (just like Dr. St. Claire taught her).

"Principal Basset, you're creating a situation where one doesn't need to exist." She spoke deliberately. "Your unwillingness to compromise is ridiculous. It's absurd."

"I think it's important for us to take a step back here."

"From what?"

Principal Basset cleared his throat. "We need to look at the reality of the situation."

"*Puh-lease.*" Mom dismissed him with a wave of her hand. "It's bad enough you've told me to *calm down.* Don't start telling me to *look at the reality of the situation.* I'm not one of your students."

"What you're asking for is against school policy."

"Are we back to that?" Mom snarled. "You said that before, and I said show me the policy." She strummed her fingers on his desk. "I'm still waiting."

"Well . . . well, it's against the spirit of the policy."

"The *spirit* of the policy? Is that the best you can come up with?" Mom hoisted herself from her chair again. "This isn't a question of school policy, and you know it. This is a question of you avoiding controversy."

Talk about hitting the nail on the head!

Principal Basset will do practically anything, and I mean *anything,* to avoid controversy. To put it mildly, the man isn't at his best during times of conflict.

Case in point: When I was a freshman, the student council submitted a two-hundred-fifty-signature petition to the school board asking to have the school's nickname changed. Finley High used to be the Frontiersmen, but no one could remember there ever being a frontier anywhere close to Finley. Plus the name's sexist suffix riled many of the students. So the student council proposed a name change from the backward and antebellum Finley Frontiersmen to the cutting-edge and postmillennial Finley Force.

Well . . .

During the seven weeks that this topic of conversation and debate divided the community (however divided a community can actually become over such a nondivisive issue), Principal Basset was a basket case on the verge of a breakdown.

"Change for the sake of change is not a reason for change," he cried over and over.

With every passing day, he looked more and more haggard, gaunt, and sleep-deprived. I swear, it got to the point where the man could barely leave his office. He simply could not deal . . . much as he was having trouble dealing at this very moment.

"I'm going to have to digest this matter further." Principal Basset picked up a pen and scribbled some notes. "I'm going to have to consult with members of the school board. They may wish to hold a hearing before I render a verdict."

Hold a hearing? Render a verdict? Who did he think he was, Judge Judy?

"What time frame are we talking about here?" Mom asked. "The longer this goes on, the more difficult this becomes. For everyone."

"I should be able to let you know within the week."

"That's fine," Nathalie replied, but she was shaking her head. "In the meantime, my daughter and I will be proceeding through alternative channels. This needs to be addressed and resolved expeditiously."

Go, Mom!

"I can't agree with you more. We need to look at the reality of the—"

"Trust me!" Nathalie cut him off. "If you force my hand with this one, I'll go over your head uttering catchphrases like equal protection, sex discrimination, and gender bias."

Don't stop now, Nathalie!

Principal Basset rubbed his temples.

Then he reached into his top desk drawer and pulled out the box of Maalox.

Then he reached back in and pulled out the container of Advil.

"I just don't understand why this isn't clearer to you." Mom was smelling blood. "Darcy's played softball the last three years. The team is awful, and she's no longer enjoying herself. Put her on the baseball team, and she'll be the best player out there—no offense to your son. The team will finally win its championship. Why is this such a problem?"

Exactly. Why is it such a problem?

All I want is to play for the baseball team.

2

After what I've had to endure, asking to play for the boys' baseball team shouldn't be such an unreasonable request.

You see, for the last three years the softball team has won a grand total of three games over three seasons (and one of those victories was by forfeit). We even became Finley's first varsity team in *any* sport to go a full season without winning when we compiled a 0–13 record my sophomore year. Needless to say, ineptitude of that magnitude takes the fun out of things.

Now comes the obvious question: If I'm so good, how come the softball team is so pathetic? We should be able to win a few games with Darcy the Ringer on the squad, right?

Uh, wrong.

You see, at the plate I'm never allowed to hit. I get intentionally walked three and four times a game. In the field I play shortstop, but there are only so many chances I can try for without my teammates hating my guts for being a total ball hog.

Now while the softball team was mired in misery, the baseball team was consistently competitive and went on great runs only to fall just short of glory and high school immortality.

When I was a freshman, the baseball team qualified for the playoffs and faced a first-round opponent they had already spanked during the regular season. Unfortunately, come playoff time, the team was—how can I put this politely?—a little cocky. This time *they* got spanked, 26–0 spanked, the county record for largest margin of victory in a playoff game.

The following season the team atoned for that opening-round playoff debacle and advanced to the division championship. To celebrate, the team's senior captain, who was also the all-world centerfielder, lights-out closer, and the team's leading base stealer, threw a massive (and now legendary) outdoor keg party. As one could expect, things got a tad rowdy and out of hand, and the party had to be broken up by the local men in blue. In the process, several players received summonses and citations, including the host, who was actually arrested for relieving himself on a police cruiser. Five starters were suspended for the championship game, and the season went down in flames.

Last year the team advanced to the championship game, but this time they publicly vowed to stay the course. No blowout beer blasts this time around. Instead, the team's coach hosted a more manageable, players-only victory barbecue. Too bad grilling burgers and dogs was not the coach's specialty. Eleven players were stricken with food poisoning, eight of whom remained hospitalized on the day of the championship.

In light of the three consecutive successful regular seasons, it's hard to argue against the notion that some form of malevolent postseason supernatural deity is at work. However, if some unseen and unknown force is *not* responsible (as improbable as that may seem), then the only other possible explanation is that each season the baseball team has simply been one superstar short. The team has been missing one key ingredient, a key ingredient that would have provided depth at key positions, stability, good karma, leadership, and a clutchness that would have for certain brought it over the top and delivered it into the promised land.

And that key ingredient?

Me.

At least that's what Nathalie was saying. And she happened to be right. And I'm not saying that to be cocky, conceited, or a bitch. It's the truth. Period.

"Give her the opportunity, and she'll lead Finley baseball to that championship. Guaranteed."

But that's Nathalie talking. When she's in one of her gone-overboard, superlative tirades, she'll shoot her mouth off and say whatever she wants no matter what I say.

I would never say stuff like that.

What would I say?

I just want to play for the baseball team. Take the field. Hear my name announced.

"Now batting: Darcy Miller."

That would be plenty. It is that simple.

All I want is to play for the baseball team.

8   Phil Bildner

3

"But the baseball team is all boys," Principal Basset continued to lamely defend his stance. "Darcy, I really think you'll be unnecessarily ruffling a lot of feathers."

"Oh, spare me your clichés," Nathalie huffed. She pointed two fingers at Principal Basset's eyes and then turned those fingers around and pointed them at herself. Translation: He was not to speak to me directly. "Principal Basset, all those boys care about is winning a championship, and you know it. They don't give a rat's ass about with whom, in what way, or how."

"Darcy," he brazenly addressed me again, "baseball is a completely different animal than softball."

I looked at Mom. She nodded her consent for me to speak.

"I'm aware of that," I said.

"Many of the most fundamental concepts are different. Pitching, defense, hitting—it's not the same."

Uh, can you say *condescending?* God, I hated his tone. I wanted to mouth off so bad, but I knew if I did, Nathalie would toss me out of the Range Rover the second we hit the interstate.

"Take running the base paths," Principal Basset went on. "What happens on a line drive?"

"*Puh-lease!*" I rolled my eyes, unable to contain myself from using Mom's signature retort. Hey, it's in the Miller genes.

Was he actually going to quiz me on baseball situations? Shit, I had *forgotten* more about baseball in my seventeen short years of existence than that man would ever know!

I clasped my hands in my lap and sat up prep-school perfect.

"Principal Basset, what a base runner does on a line drive in both baseball *and* softball all depends on the number of outs. With less than two outs, a runner waits for the line drive to leave the infield to avoid getting doubled off. Of course, the exception in baseball occurs when the hit-and-run is on. With the hit-and-run, the baseball runner is off when the pitcher makes his move toward home plate, so if a line drive happens to be hit directly at an infielder, the baseball runner will be doubled-off. In softball the runner may leave as soon as the ball leaves the pitcher's hand, so on a line drive they will do their best to return to the base before being doubled-off. Now if there are two outs, on a line drive or on *any* batted ball, in both baseball *and* softball, the runner is off with the crack of the bat." I cracked my knuckles for sound-effect emphasis. "Does that answer your question?"

"Darcy, there's . . . there's . . . there's more to this." Principal Basset's flustered expression was precious. "A girl can't play on a boys' varsity team. We need to look at the reality of this situation." He said the phrase without even realizing it.

"Are we back to that?" Mom huffed again. "I'm tired of talking in circles here. We're getting absolutely nowhere." She stood up. "Is there anything new you wish to add, Principal Basset?" She said his name with the perfect amount of sass.

"Not at this time."

"Then I believe we're done." Mom motioned for me to stand. "Come, Darcy."

Phil Bildner

I stood to leave and nearly walked right into her as she suddenly pivoted around at the door.

"I'm marinating chicken," Nathalie said, now wearing one of her glowingly sickening expressions. "I'll see you about seven? Seven-thirty?"

The relief on Principal Basset's face was comical.

"Um, er, sure, Nathalie. About seven. Seven works."

"Wonderful." She smiled and blew a kiss to her temporary adversary now turned back into her boyfriend of the last six months. "See you then."

She sailed out the door. And as I slunk out after her, that all-too-familiar nausea settled back into that place in my gut where it had been residing for the last half year.

You see, my mom and my high school principal are dating. Yes, that's right. My mom, my principal, dating. But don't worry; it's not as bad as it seems.

It's worse. Much worse.

How much worse?

Well, right now I'm sitting in *my* corner of the Finley High School student lounge, along the windows and next to the Snapple machine, and as I look around at all the juniors and seniors in here with me (the lounge is a restricted-access area, off-limits to newbies, sophs, *and* teachers), there isn't a single one who doesn't know far more than they need to about my ghastly situation.

This "situation" developed last fall, and that budding romance— which Nathalie attempted to keep from me for the first month—has been the source of some serious mother-daughter tension. At times, we've gone at it something fierce. We're talking shut-the-windows-lower-the-shades-remove-all-sharp-objects-from-the-immediate-vicinity-no-holds-barred brouhahas.

I mean, let's be reasonable here: Being branded the Girl Whose Mom Is Doing the Principal is not exactly the label of choice for *any* senior, let alone a senior with a favorable ranking on the high school popularity chart. A girl's going to take some serious shit, and trust me, kids—even those many links beneath you on the high school food chain—have no qualms about calling it like they see it.

As soon as word got out, I was fair game. Overnight!

I had *freshmen* giggling past me in the hallway, and they didn't even try masking it behind a cupped hand or notebook like they usually do when they laugh in someone's face.

And you should have seen some of the wonderful photographs of Nathalie and Bill that started to magically appear—slipped into my gym locker, thumbtacked to a bulletin board, taped to my hall locker, tucked under my wiper blades. Let's just say kids can be very creative with even limited digital-imaging skills.

Even the freakin' lunch lady got in on the action! She put condoms on my lunch tray—between the fruit cocktail and the tossed salad—and attached a love note that read: "Adults are people too. Talk to your parents about safe sex."

Oh, that's comedy.

About as funny as when the editors of the *Finley Final Word*, our esteemed high school newspaper, decided to chip in *their* two cents. A headline in their anything-goes April Fools' Day edition screamed NATHALIE THE NYMPH BOPS BILL THE BACHELOR.

A real laugh riot.

Let me tell you, it gets mad old DSL-fast—especially when the abuse and antics aren't limited to the confines of your high school. Yes, this nonsense even jumped the firewalls, and I had the pleasure of receiving e-mails and IMs from kids at neighboring schools. Kids I didn't even know!

Now when something like this happens to you in high school (and pray hard it doesn't), it's life-altering. It requires you to change some friendships and relationships, and in my case, I'm specifically referring to my friendship and relationship with Brandon Basset.

Brandon Basset, the boy of my dreams.

Brandon is the principal's son, and suffice it to say, his mere existence raises a most provocative question: Which is worse—having your dad as your high school principal or having your mom *date* your high school principal?

But I digress.

Brandon is the shortstop and senior captain of the varsity baseball team. He's one of those "gifted" or "special" kids who's allowed to get away with things. Why? Because he's perfect, the perfect teenage male (obviously, his dominant genes do not generate from his father's side). Every high school has a handful of Brandons—looks, charm, wit, popularity, athletic ability, coolness, Jeep convertible—and those that fit this mold are afforded certain societal privileges that we ordinary people don't merit.

Brandon also happens to be my friend. Well, he used to be, anyway, and I'll even go so far as to say he had become *more* than a friend.

Brandon and I had one of those complex, makes-no-sense friendship-relationships. Sometimes we'd chill together at a party, or end up in the same late-night group in somebody's basement or yard or deck or hot tub, but other times we wouldn't speak for days or even say hi when we passed each other in the hall.

I liked Brandon—no, I *really* liked Brandon—but I never thought I had a chance. I always thought he was, well, out of my league.

At least until last summer's random encounter at the food court. And I do mean random. Come on, what are the chances that I would be at the mall *by myself* and Brandon would also be at the mall *by himself* at the same time? I admit it was one of those brutally hot July afternoons when people go to air-conditioned malls to escape the heat, but considering that I can count on one hand and have fingers left over the number of times in my existence I've been to the mall by myself, the odds against this chance interaction were Powerball out-of-this-world.

At any rate, we literally bumped into each other on the down escalator, and then somehow ended up spending hours, actual hours, sitting and talking—and eating a half dozen mountain-sized orders of cheese fries so greasy and nasty that my pores still haven't fully recovered.

But let me tell you, it was worth every blemish and blackhead.

Because of what Brandon said to me:

"Darcy, I've always wanted to spend time with you alone." He paused for dramatic effect or to gather his nerve.

"But you're always with your friends." He paused for dramatic effect or to gather his nerve again.

"Or I'm always with mine, or there's always other people around." He bit on the corner of his lower lip—to die for! I started to melt.

"There's something different about you, Darcy."

His words. Verbatim.

You can't begin to imagine—or maybe you can—the wonders that did for the self-esteem!

Now to the untrained observer, Brandon didn't say much of anything, but anyone with any inkling and insight into the workings of the teenage mind knows this was a breakthrough moment.

Honest. It was. I know what I'm talking about.

Well, after that midsummer's afternoon dream, Brandon and I started to engage in this semi-ritualistic dance, this several week–long flirtation thing that was so silly, but so sexy. But for some reason, it didn't go anywhere. Nothing happened. And it was going to. I *know* it was, if not for the tragic, horror-show parental arrangement that came to life. At which point anything that did exist or may have happened was shot to hell in a heartbeat.

I instantly imposed a no-fly zone, and Brandon understood and obliged. We mutually agreed to stop interacting. If we were seen together—even if we were spotted trading glances—it would only add fuel to this fire, and trust me, these were flames that didn't need to be fanned.

Fun stuff, right?

The Nathalie-Bill relationship recently celebrated its six-month anniversary, but the initial shock and horror of this union has yet to fully wear off. However—and I can't believe I'm about to go here—close study and analysis of the situation have led me to a shocking conclusion: Bill Basset isn't all bad.

Now a few months ago, I would've never been able to say that, so either I've been abducted by aliens, or brainwashed, or as Nathalie likes to say, "Darcy, I think you're finally growing up."

Puh-lease.

Let me try to explain. First of all, Principal Basset's got a pretty decent body for a man pushing the big five-uh-oh. He's very athletic, and through this warped convergence of my home and school lives, I've learned he's run several marathons and a couple of triathalons.

It also doesn't hurt that Principal Basset is loaded, and I mean, loaded. But don't start thinking he's some money mogul. His money is family money (but to be quite honest, in my eyes, *dinero* is *dinero*). The man drives a Jag *and* a Lexus SUV, owns a beautiful five-bedroom home, and vacations several times a year either in the Caribbean or the Mediterranean. He also regularly digs into his own pocket to help underwrite or subsidize school functions and kid-oriented causes.

Phil Bildner

Bill also loves children. Well, duh, he *is* a high school principal. One would consider that a job requirement. But Bill goes above and beyond the call of duty. He does some genuinely altruistic things for kids that I've never seen *any* other adult do.

For instance, at the beginning of each school year, Principal Basset holds a pediatric cancer fund-raiser. Translation: Principal Basset is a principal who sponsors a charitable event where the financial proceeds do not go to *his* school. But the school does in fact receive some benefit because nearly every Finley student gets involved in the community-building effort. It also doesn't hurt that participation counts toward — and completes most of — our community-service requirements for the entire semester.

Principal Basset also coordinates the Holiday Burn Force. (Note the clever usage of Finley's new nickname.) Each December, the Finley student service organizations travel to inner-city after-school programs, group homes, and religious organizations to ask kids what their favorite songs are and who their favorite artists are. Then back at school, the student groups burn customized CDs, which then get distributed as Christmas gifts (for the sake of the cause, any and all copyright infringement issues are discarded, overlooked, and ignored).

There are other things Principal Basset does as well, but on a smaller scale. He holds before- and after-school extra-help sessions during midterms and finals. He provides the adult supervision one evening each week and one Saturday morning each month so that students in good standing can use the main gym or the pool area. He . . .

Wait.

Hold the phone!

I'm creating a picture of Saint Bill Basset! No, no, no. Bill

Basset does not get glorified. No way. Things need to be presented accurately. We are talking about my high school principal; we are talking about the goofball who is dating my mom; we are talking about the same guy who . . .

Bill Basset is plenty bizarre, and some of his neuroses are downright disconcerting. For instance, Bill Basset has this weird *B* obsession; I guess you can call it that. Of course, his last name begins with the letter *B*, but for some reason every Basset has a first name beginning with *B* as well. Principal Basset is William, but he goes by Bill. His ex-wife is Bonnie, and I'm sure the *beginning* of her name was a prerequisite to their dating in the first place. Bill and Bonnie have three children: Brandon, and twin seventh graders, Brian and Brenda.

The Bassets divorced several years ago, and to his credit Bachelor Bill may finally be evolving—and considering how much he hates change, that's nothing short of miraculous. Bill's *B* psychosis may be waning because he's now with Nathalie, and if the two ever decide to take their relationship to another level . . .

Longdeeplongdeeplongdeep breath.

Another disturbing aspect to Bill Basset's persona is his appearance. He needs to do something about that hair and those teeth. Quickly! His short, graying, unkempt hair is so oily it looks like his head hijacked Iran, and his compulsive coffee drinker's teeth are as yellow as the tiles around a nursery school urinal.

Then there's his fashion sense, or lack thereof. A high school principal resides in one of the most fashionably vulnerable positions known to humankind. Every student is Joan and Melissa Rivers. Fashion judgment should be of utmost concern. But not for Principal Braindead. His wardrobe's as predictable as the cast of *Gilligan's Island*.

Principal Basset also likes to go running after school on the track around the football field. How clueless can one man be? Does he not realize people watch? His running attire is mortifying. We're talking fluorescent yellow and neon orange spandex—which fits so snugly it leaves absolutely nothing to the imagination.

Ah, that's more like it! That's a much fairer and much more accurate portrayal of the man who's doing the nasty with my mom. As you can see, there's plenty awry with Bill Basset.

But yes, I know he's good to my mom. In the end, that's all that matters. Because if he wasn't good to her, I'd have to kill him.

Kill Principal Basset?

Hmmm.

No, wishful thinking.

5

Two mornings after the fateful meeting with Principal Basset, I awoke to find a kitchen-table Post-it from Nathalie. I couldn't exactly claim I didn't see this one (as I've been known to do in the past) because today's communication was strategically attached to the salt shaker, atop the stack of ten days' worth of newspapers I had neglected to place in the recycling bin.

Now whenever Nathalie leaves me kitchen-table notes, I get nervous. It's her method of delivering bad news. You see, Nathalie isn't very good with face-to-face, mother-daughter exchanges, so she usually eases into them via the Post-it. It's how she kinda-sorta informed me about her first three dates with Principal Basset; it's how she kinda-sorta told me I couldn't go to the junior prom because I was grounded for smoking *her* pot in the basement; and it's how she kinda-sorta started to break the news that she killed my dog Legsy (okay, it was an accident, but I still say she killed her, and no matter what, a stickie is no way to break the news to anyone that their dog is dead).

Well, the note du jour told me to go see Principal Basset some-time that day. I instantly freaked. Don't know why. Just did.

So like anybody who is having a moment, I called my best friend. Samantha.

"I'm having a crisis."

"Why are you calling me at this hour?"

Ah, she can be so compassionate.

"Sam, I'm having a crisis."

"You didn't answer my question."

Sam isn't exactly what you'd call a morning person. Nor is sensitivity one of her strong suits.

"We have school in fifteen minutes, Sam. Aren't you going?"

"Aren't you going to answer my question?"

Years of experience enabled me to realize the futility of this conversation, so instead of getting frustrated and annoyed, I pushed End. Sam and I would deal with this later. For now, I was going to have to deal with the latest Principal Basset situation on my own.

Of course, I opted to deal during my math test. Hey, the principal needed to see me, and I couldn't disobey the principal. Nor could I think of a better time.

Well, the moment he saw me, he hung up the phone and leaped out of his seat.

"Darcy! I'm glad you made it."

He hugged me and kissed the top of my head.

Eww! I nearly fell out.

"Please, Darcy. Come in. Sit down."

I sat in the same chair Mom had been sitting in a couple of days earlier and eyed him skeptically. Something was up. Something was definitely up.

For one thing, he was smiling that same pathetically forced grin he greets me with whenever I have the pleasure of seeing him these days in the kitchen of *my* house on mornings after he has spent the night with . . .

Double eww.

There isn't a Costco-sized vat of Preparation H large enough to soothe such levels of burning discomfort.

"I never knew, Darcy. I had no idea."

Okay, what the hell are you talking about?

"It all makes perfect sense now." He rolled his chair around his desk. "You're one brave young lady."

I nodded doubtfully.

"Darcy, if I had known, I would have never resisted like I did." He rolled to a stop in front of me and smiled uncomfortably. "Of course . . . of course you can play baseball."

Run that by me one more time. I can?

"I mean, you'll have to try out and all, just like any normal . . . er . . . uh . . . any other player, but from what I understand . . . from what I understand, you won't have any problem." He exhaled audibly. "I'm so ashamed of my behavior with you and Nathalie on Monday. It's all I've been able to think about."

"Why was it bothering you so much?" I figured if I asked the right question, I could learn why he was suddenly giving me the green light on baseball.

"Well, it can be a very sensitive subject area. Especially with high school students."

"You think so?"

"Certainly." He still smiled his pathetically forced and uncomfortable smile. He rolled in closer. "Darcy, I have so many questions."

Not as many questions as I have, Bill!

"For one thing, when did you first realize it?"

I shrugged. "I've been thinking about it awhile."

"Really. How long's awhile?"

"I think it first hit me sitting in the bleachers last spring. During the playoffs."

"Interesting." Principal Basset stroked his chin. "It came to you just like that?"

"I guess so." I shrugged again. "I just realized I was playing on the wrong field."

Principal Basset forced a laugh. "That's one way of putting it!"

Okay, this conversation was now officially surreal. I felt like I had somehow been transported into a *Friends* rerun where Joey was talking about one thing and Phoebe was talking about another, and the lone miscommunication formed the basis of Monica, Ross, Chandler, and Rachel's confusion and the show's entire half-hour plotline.

"Darcy, I'm proud of you. I really am. It takes a courageous individual to do what you're doing. Many people don't act on this until much later in life, if they act on it at all."

This is driving me insane! What the hell are you talking about?

"But Darcy, I do have a confession to make," Principal Basset paused. "I am rather ashamed about the way I found out."

"Found out?"

"I hope you're not going to be too angry." He paused again. "Brandon's the one who told me why you want to play baseball."

Brandon? What does Brandon know?

"He's the one who told me. He's the one who told me that you're g-g- . . . well, you know."

I nodded doubtfully again.

Principal Basset's uneasy smile resurfaced. "I think it's called . . . it's called outing, when someone reveals that another person is g-g- . . . or a le-les- . . . when someone divulges another person's sexual orientation." He paused yet again before admitting, "Some people don't think it's a very nice thing to do."

6

A lesbian.

Principal Basset thinks I'm a lesbian. That's what Brandon told him. That's why I can play baseball.

What is *that*?

Since when does being a lesbian suddenly make someone eligible for boys' baseball? What kind of ass-backward, anachronistic (SAT word) way of thinking is that? This is twenty-first-century suburbia, not Reaganville circa 1987.

I'm a lesbian? What the hell is Brandon trying to pull?

Darcy, I've always wanted to spend time with you alone. But you're always with your friends. Or I'm always with mine, or there's always other people around. There's something different about you, Darcy.

That little shit! Who does he think he is, spreading lies like that? He's got no business speaking about me *period*.

Longdeeplongdeeplongdeep breath.

And knowing Brandon, I know this lesbian-Darcy thing isn't just some shared father-son piece of inside information. This is in circulation, in heavy rotation among his posse of pretty boys and pretty-boy wannabes. No doubt, this is out there. Oh, it's out there.

Stay calm, Darcy.

Longdeeplongdeeplongdeep breath.

This isn't as bad as it seems. You'll get to the bottom of this, Darcy.

Longdeeplongdeeplongdeep breath.

Hey, this breathing thing actually works! Thanks, Dr. St. Claire! In fact . . .

Hold the phone. I'm a lesbian? Okay, fine. I'm a lesbian.

If Principal Braindead and his pretty boy wonder want to think that, then so be it. But make no mistake, I'm going to figure out what the hell is going on here, and when I do, I'm going to get the upper hand with the *both* of them.

Yes, Darcy Miller, newly minted lesbian Darcy Miller, will play baseball no matter what the situation.

Situations don't dictate Darcy Miller. Darcy Miller dictates situations.

"Darcy? Darcy? Are you okay?" Principal Basset shook my shoulder.

"Huh? Yeah, fine." I had completely tuned him out during my "so-now-I'm-a-lesbian" mind meander. "I'm fine."

"Did you hear what I said?"

"Uh, actually, no. Can you say it again?"

"I said, some of the less enlightened students at Finley may give you a hard time. You realize that, don't you?"

Duh. Like I'm not already hearing it with you dating my mom.

"I know."

"And I want you to know my door is always open. If you have any problems, if anyone gives you a hard time, or if you just want to talk, I'm always here for you."

Oh, puke.

"Thank you."

"I've already spoken to Coach Irving about this. He'll be expecting you at baseball practice. I'll just remind him again this afternoon."

"Thank you," I said again.

"Now I do have a few questions."

Join the club.

"Have you said anything to your mother?"

"No!" My eyes exploded. "God, no. You haven't talked to her about this, have you?"

"Oh, no. Never. I promise. I wanted to discuss it with you first."

"Thank you." I placed a hand on my chest. Nathalie couldn't find out about this second- or third-hand. I needed to break my newfound lesbianism to her. "It's a sensitive topic," I added.

"I completely understand. This is something she'll need to accept at her own pace."

"But Principal Basset, Nathalie's going to want to know what happened. What changed your mind? Why are you suddenly letting me play? She'll grill you. You know she will."

"I've given this a lot of thought." Principal Basset rolled his chair back around his desk and sat down across from me. "I'm going to need your help."

I didn't like the sound of that.

He leaned in. "I don't think Nathalie needs to know the reasoning behind my allowing you to play baseball."

"You're going to keep a secret from Nathalie?"

"Well, I wouldn't exactly put it that way. I'm simply trying to . . . trying to minimize controversy." He forced a laugh. "I care for your mother very deeply, Darcy. I think you know that."

And the nausea returns.

"I would never speak badly of her in any setting, but your mother thrives on chaos and controversy, and I think if she feels I'm letting you play because of some fear of that, she'll be quite perturbed."

"I don't understand."

I wasn't trying to be difficult (like I usually am). I didn't understand what he was getting at.

"Sexuality is such a sensitive topic with so many people." He leaned in farther. "I think it's best if we try to keep this low-key."

"I don't know. Nathalie has this thing about honesty."

"Yes, you're a hundred percent correct, Darcy. She certainly does. Nathalie's a stickler for honesty. It's one of the qualities I love most about her."

Seriously. He needed to stop.

Did he really have to use the four letter l-word in the same breath as my mom's name?

"But I'm afraid that if your mother finds out the only reason I'm letting you play is because of your sexuality . . ." Principal Basset shook his head to finish the thought.

"I don't know. I feel like I'm duping my own mother. I'm not sure if I like this."

"Darcy, I completely understand." Principal Basset folded his arms and rocked back in his chair. "But at least for now, I'm going to leave your sexuality out of the equation. If Nathalie asks why I finally decided to let you play, I'm simply going to say there's no reason why you shouldn't. I'm going to tell her she was right. I think that'll satisfy her."

I have to admit Principal Basset was making some genuinely valid points. If Nathalie knew the real reason why he was letting me play, she would make such a stink over it that the whole situation could backfire miserably. For everyone.

Still, I knew there had to be more to this, but like every other thirteen- to seventeen-year-old who ever walked the corridors of a high school, I knew better than to try to figure out the thought process of an educrat. I mean, how do you even try explaining ending school last year on a Monday? Did they really think kids *and* teachers were going to show up? And how do you even try explaining a zero-tolerance chewing-gum policy when all three school vending machines still sell Blow Pops?

Got me.

No, you don't even attempt to attach any form of logical reasoning to decision-making of this sort. Simply accept the stupidity and insanity and incongruity and whatever else you want to call it, and high school becomes . . . high school.

For real. Pretty numbing stuff.

So my being a lesbian couldn't create insta baseball-team eligibility—or could it?

"Darcy, I think by now you've come to realize your mother and I have a very special relationship."

No! Nasty!

I didn't need to hear this. It was bad enough I had to endure mush-tales from Nathalie on the home front. No way was I going to have to listen to them coming from Bill sitting in his office!

Suddenly, I hated this. I felt like a pawn, and making matters even worse, I was working in cahoots with Principal Basset. We were going to be partners in crime. But what choice did I really have? I wanted to play baseball, and yes, when it came down to it, it was as simple as that.

"So if we do it this way, I don't think Nathalie will be an issue, and your le-les- . . . that will never come up."

"Principal Basset, you can say it," I blurted out.

"Excuse me?"

"You can say the word. It's not a slur."

"What's not?"

"The l-word. Lesbian. It's not a slur."

Principal Basset's cheeks reddened. He dabbed his brow.

"I'm a lesbian," I said proudly. "It's not an insult. It's who I am."

He nodded quickly. "Oh, I know that."

No, actually, he *didn't* know that, and I wanted him to know I didn't appreciate his reaction.

"You make it seem like I'm lesser," I said.

"No . . . I—"

"Does it make me lesser?"

Principal Basset's face went from tomato to full Casper. "Um . . . no . . . no, of course, I don't. I think . . . I think . . ." He squirmed in his seat. "Which brings me to my next point."

"What's that?"

Principal Basset shakily stood up and rolled his chair around his desk once again. He opened up a folder, removed a sheet of paper, and sat back down. "Darcy, I'd like for you to consider something."

"Okay." I didn't like the sudden shift in his tone.

"I'd like for you to join the GSA."

"Excuse me?"

"The GSA. It's a student organization here at Finley."

"Principal Basset, I know what the GSA is."

"A growing number of schools now have one." He continued like he had practiced these exact words and he couldn't be interrupted. "It's an organization for students with . . . with . . . with alternative lifestyles and those who support them. The students—"

"Principal Basset, I said I know what the GSA is."

"Good. Oh, good. Then I'd like for you to join."

That's what I thought he said.

Principal Basset was asking me to join the Gay-Straight Alliance! Correction, Principal Basset was *telling* me to join the Gay-Straight Alliance.

"But rest assured, Darcy, no one will know that you're . . . that you're . . ."

Principal Basset still couldn't get himself to say the words "gay" and "lesbian," but I was no longer enjoying his uneasiness. I was experiencing shock and panic and discomfort of my own.

"I'm going to have Brandon join as well."

Gulp.

"In fact, I'd like you two to go together."

Double gulp.

"But Brandon's not g-g-. . . . Brandon's heterosexual, of course. He's . . . he's . . ." Principal Basset stammered and smiled his smile.

"Of course," I murmured.

"Darcy, you understand this presents a unique opportunity for tolerance here at Finley. I'm sure you of all people understand that."

"I do understand that." I could feel myself starting to sweat. "But I'm not so sure this is such a good idea right away."

"If the GSA has two members of the baseball team join the organization, it will do wonders for the group's morale."

"We need to look at the reality of the situation." I resorted to his time-tested approach.

But he wasn't having it. Principal Basset's mind was made up.

"Two members of the baseball team!" He clapped his hands. "One straight and one . . . one not straight, even though that doesn't matter. Think . . . think of the wonderful effect this will have on the entire community."

Wonderful effect? Oh, no. This had disaster written all over it.

8

Wow.

I was numb.

Back in my spot by the Snapple machine in my corner of the student lounge, I tried to digest what the hell had just happened. But I couldn't think straight. Well, of course I couldn't think straight—supposedly I no longer *was* straight!

Longdeeplongdeeplongdeep breath.

Brandon.

That little shit! Telling his dad I'm a lesbian. Who did he think he was? Why would he say that? No way was he getting away with this. This went too far. He and I were going to have a little talk. And soon. Next time I saw that puss-boy—and I don't care where it was—I was going to be all over him.

Longdeeplongdeeplongdeep breath.

The student lounge wasn't working for me. Too many people were seeing me upset, and they knew it had something to do with my mom and the principal, even though this time it didn't, but it did, only in a totally new way.

I needed to be alone. Fast. I was going to lose my shit if I didn't get the hell out of there.

I can't believe this is happening. I can't believe this is happening.

I stood up to leave, but immediately sat back down. I wasn't going *anywhere*. I was trapped.

Josh. Oh God, Josh!

What was I thinking? I knew he was free now, and he always comes to the lounge during his free periods. Way to go, Darcy.

You see, Josh is my best friend. Well, my ex–best friend. We're not exactly on speaking terms these days, and when we do talk, it's not exactly pleasant.

Josh is gay. Not pretend gay like me, really gay. In fact, Josh is the reason why I got so pissed at Principal Basset when he couldn't even get himself to say the g-word or the l-word. Josh is responsible for teaching me all about tolerance and ignorance, and no matter what the status of our friendship, I will always love him for that.

Josh also happens to be founder and president of GSA. Yes, that's the same GSA that Principal Braindead is making Brandon and me join. Of course, the main reason Josh and I are no longer civil to one another is directly related to his involvement with GSA, specifically his ever-increasing tendency to take everything and anything even tangentially related to his sexuality way too seriously.

So trust me, when Josh finds out about all this, things are going to get ugly. He is going to Mount St. Helens lose it!

See why I'm buggin'? Pieces falling into place yet?

Longdeeplongdeeplongdeep breath.

But factoring Josh into this whole mess was going to have to wait. I couldn't allow myself to go there. My head would explode. Right now, I needed to get the hell out of the student lounge.

So I mustered up the courage to leave, which entailed walking right past him as he sat by himself eating a slice of pizza and reading *Teen People* or *Us Weekly*.

"Hanging out with all your friends?" I asked.

I couldn't help myself. Despite my desperate condition, I couldn't resist the dig. More than likely he would've said something to me anyway, so I figured I might as well fire the first shot.

"BSB," he muttered without looking up.

BSB—that's what Josh has taken to calling me. It stands for Back-Stabbing Bitch.

"We're going to need to talk," I said.

Josh still didn't look up. But he did raise his middle finger at me before shoveling the slice of pizza into his mouth.

"School pizza, Josh? Let's see, if two slices of Pizza Hut pepperoni has two hundred fat calories, just imagine what you're ingesting right now."

"BSB, don't you have anything better to do? Why don't you find some other friend to abandon?"

I hated it whenever he said I abandoned him. Because I didn't. I was always there for him. Just like he had always been there for me. No matter what he says now. Even after our Three Mile Island meltdown. He knows that. He has to. He just says I abandoned him because he's hurt.

We both are.

"Seriously, Josh, we do need to talk."

"Seriously, BSB, you need to go straight to hell."

"I need you to meet me in the playground tonight."

"Do you not get it? I do not want you in my world anymore. How many times do I have to tell you that?"

"Josh, this is important." I tried to stay calm.

"Oh, excuse me! Because you say something's important, it's important. But when something was important to me, it didn't mean shit. What you did to me was unforgivable. Friends don't do that to friends. So I've moved on. These last few months without you in my life have been the most wonder—"

"Josh, the playground tonight," I interrupted.

"BSB, which word didn't you understand?" Josh slammed his hand on the table. "I no longer acknowledge your existence. Is that clear enough for you?"

Josh had not moved on. Not by any stretch.

You see, when my dad picked up and left Nathalie and me on my twelfth birthday, I nearly fell apart (although compared to Nathalie, I was a pillar of stability). If it wasn't for Josh, I don't know how I would have survived. He was a friend in every sense, and I promised I would be there for him in the same way if he ever needed me.

That's a big part of why our "breakup" hurt Josh more than me (although trust me, it hurt me plenty too). Hands down, I was the most important person in his life.

I was the first person Josh ever came out to. He did it at the end of freshman year. I mean, we both knew he was gay, but I was the first person he *officially* told.

At the time, sexuality speaking, he was a mess, a total wreck, a basket case, whatever you want to call it. We're talking he needed *me* to take him to the gay & lesbian section at Barnes & Noble. He wouldn't even look at gay porn on the net, not even with his bedroom door double-bolted, his mother at work, and his dad in Europe on business!

I was there for him every step of the way. Just like I said I would be. In fact, in a lot of ways I came out *with* him (although if that's the case, I'm about to come out all over again).

Well, Josh and I had the most amazing sophomore year. We did everything together, and it was so cool to watch my best friend go through this metamorphosis. Josh changed from this uncertain closet case into this kid amazingly comfortable in his skin.

When you experience something like that with someone, and then you lose that person, it hurts. A lot.

"Listen, Josh," I began to plead, "this has to do with you, the GSA, and Brandon."

Suddenly I had his attention. My last sentence contained all the magic words, considering the GSA was his baby, and Brandon was the boy he fantasized about calling baby. Yes, Josh and I shared the boy of our dreams, and let me tell you, that made for some pretty amusing and explicit conversations.

"The playground. Tonight, Josh. I have baseball practice until—"

"Yeah, I heard Basset's letting you play baseball."

How could he possibly know? News does not travel *that* fast. Not even at Finley.

Josh was shaking his head. "What's that all about?"

"How do you know?"

"Walls can talk. What's *that* all about?" he repeated.

I couldn't have this conversation.

"There's a lot to it, Josh. I can't get into it right now."

"Ah, BSB, up to her same manipulative, bullshit antics." Josh sucked the tomato sauce off his teeth.

"The playground, Josh," I said for the fourth time. "Around ten." I started heading away, but turned back. "That won't interfere with your reruns of *Will & Grace*, will it?"

Way too early and still wearing my street clothes, I headed out to baseball practice. I should've been nervous as all hell, but I wasn't. I still hadn't completely regained the ability to experience sensation as a result of the numbing events of the morning.

My mind was in overdrive. Even though I of all people knew better than to obsess over educratic decision-making, I couldn't help myself. For the life of me, I couldn't make sense of the logic allowing me to play, and I needed to know that logic, and if I didn't learn that logic, I . . .

I needed an escape. Stat!

I crossed behind the tennis courts and headed toward the practice fields located between the upper soccer fields and the track oval. I was in search of Coach Irving.

Coach Irving, or just plain Irv as he is more commonly known, is a damn good baseball coach. He's compiled a .700 winning percentage over the past three seasons, and has a lifetime win-loss record that ranks him among the tops in the state.

Irv wasn't difficult to find. He was in the middle of a hissy fit.

Now without question, watching Irv throw a tantrum is one of the best forms of entertainment money doesn't have to buy. His fits are legendary, so you can understand my disappointment that I hadn't seen this one from its inception. Still, I don't think I missed any of the good parts, but if I had, they must have been spectacular, because the ranting and raving taking place before me was quite impressive.

"Who does he think he is?" Irv kicked over the bats propped against the fence. "His son plays short, and he thinks that gives him the right to put kids on *my* team! Probably giving me some alcoholic klepto." He spun around, swept the paper cups lined up on the second row of the bleachers into the air, and then pounded his open hand on the aluminum. "Making me play politics. Damn principal thinks he's George Friggin' Steinbrenner and Jerry Friggin' Reinsdorf rolled into one." He flung his cap toward the pitcher's mound and then fired his pack of sunflower seeds into the outfield.

"Um, excuse me, Irv."

Irv bent over to pick up the watercooler, but it was too full to lift. He clutched his lower back and grimaced. "Aren't you at the wrong field?"

Like everyone associated with Finley sports, Irv knew who I was on account of my softball exploits.

But I wasn't given time to respond to his query.

"Darcy!" a voice called. "Come up here!"

I turned. Irv's brother sat on the far-side bleachers waving me over.

Irv doesn't coach the varsity team by himself. His brother, Bro, serves as the pitching coach, and most people in the know feel he's the real baseball brains behind the operation. Bro pitched in college, and he played Single-A ball in both the Dodgers and Diamondbacks organizations, but his first love was always the family's butcher business. Go figure. So Bro opted for the meat route and settled for assistant high school baseball coach on the side.

Phil Bildner

I climbed up the bleachers and sat down beside him.

"Howdy, Lassie," Bro said.

"What's wrong with Irv?" I had momentarily forgotten that Bro liked to refer to members of the female gender as "Lassie." He also tended to speak like a nineteenth-century backwoodsman with a southern drawl.

"Shucks, he's all bent outer shape 'cause Basset's dumpin' some new player on his squad."

Gulp.

"Reckon, Basset only told him 'bout it this here aft'noon."

Double gulp.

This afternoon? Braindead told me he had already spoken to Irv, and he only needed to *remind* him I was coming.

"Bro, will you excuse me for a minute?"

I had to do this now. I made my way back down the bleachers, and more confidently than I should have, walked back over to Irv by the first base coach's box.

"What are you still doing here, Darcy?"

"So how do you want to work this?" I asked.

"Work what?" Irv sneered.

"Me."

"You? What are you talking about, Darcy?"

Longdeeplongdeeplongdeep breath.

"Irv, I'm your new player."

"Come again?" Irv held his head.

"I'm the new player. Principal Basset was supposed to have told you."

"I don't think so."

"Seriously, Irv."

"Seriously, Darcy. I don't think so." Irv folded his arms on his

Santa Claus belly and brought a hand to his chin. He stared distantly out toward the infield and began to nod. "Now it makes sense."

"What does?"

"He said my new player was different." Irv still didn't look my way.

"Different? That's what he told you?" I could feel the blood rush through my veins. I wanted to take Principal Braindead by the throat and . . .

"On top of all the other crap I'm forced to put up with, now I have to allow for girls on the boys' baseball team. What's next?"

I had a million comebacks for that opening, but I opted for silence over smart-ass. A prudent choice.

"He told me I was getting a new player." Irv twirled one end of the handlebar mustache that he could never quite get to curl. "Said he had to play. Could've sworn he said *he*."

"Knowing Basset, he probably did. He say anything else?"

"He may have, but I was too busy telling him to stick it where the sun don't shine." Irv finally faced me. "Told him whatever else he had to say would only piss me off even more." A smile of resignation finally crept onto Irv's face. "Well, I'm embarrassed. Sorry 'bout my little performance."

"You didn't know," I said.

"I'll say I didn't know!" Irv refolded his arms on his belly and raised a hand to his chin again. "So what position you play? I know you play short on the soft—"

"I pitch."

"Well, don't think for a second I'm inserting you into my rotation just because Bill Basset got some bug up his ass."

"Oh, of course. I know that. I wouldn't expect you to. I didn't mean to sound like I was telling you how to coach. All I was saying—"

"All I was saying is things don't work like that 'round here,

Phil Bildner

despite what Basset thinks. You want a spot in my rotation, you'll have to earn that spot."

"Oh, of course. I know that." Then I added flatly, "But I do pitch better than everyone in your rotation."

Irv smiled. "Like the confidence, but Bro and I will be the judge of that. You'll have a tryout just like every other player on this roster."

"Oh, of course. I know that. And when I don't pitch, I play short."

As you might be able to tell, when it comes to playing ball, I know exactly what I want, and I also know exactly what to do. When you have the coach's ear, you take advantage of the situation. You ooze confidence, drive, and desire. That's what a coach wants to see and hear the moment you take the field. And this was my first moment. My skills would speak for themselves. That was a given. Right now, I was letting Irv know that in Darcy Miller, he was getting the complete package.

"We already got a shortstop," Irv said. "Brandon plays short."

"I'm better."

"You'll have to prove that, too."

"Oh, of course, I know that. But I do go to both my left *and* my right better than any shortstop in this conference."

"I'll need to see it to believe it."

"Of course. I'm not expecting you to insert me into your lineup as your starting shortstop simply because Bill Basset got some bug up his ass." I couldn't hide my smile. "Things don't work like that 'round here."

Irv exhaled a laugh. "Well, then, maybe Bill Basset was right about one thing for a change."

"What's that?" I asked.

"He said my new player was gonna ruffle a few feathers. He sure got that right." Irv scratched his forehead. "Any of the guys on the team know about this?"

"Just Brandon. As far as I know."

"Figures. He know you like to play short?"

"Not yet."

Irv chuckled. "That'll come as a nice surprise."

I nodded. "So should I get changed for practice?"

"No way! I ain't lettin' you practice today. I need a day. You'll try out tomorrow in front of the entire team. Last thing I need is my players thinkin' you're getting some kinda free pass or some kind of preferential treatment just because your . . . your mother . . . and the . . . and the principal are . . . are . . ."

Irv stopped. A gleam appeared in his eye.

"I tell you what I'm going to do, Darcy. This afternoon I'm going to let Brandon tell his teammates about their new player. And while that's happening, me and Basset Sr. are gonna have us a little confronta . . . conversation." He pointed at me. "Tomorrow. My boys are going to need a few moments when they learn their new teammate is a she-mate."

Wow.

I couldn't help but smile. This was real. This was happening. I could do this. Damn right I could do this. I could pull this off.

And something already told me Irv knew it too.

I could play for the varsity baseball team. Take the field. Hear my name announced.

"Now batting: Darcy Miller."

Phil Bildner

10

I called Samantha on the way home, but she didn't have her cell on because she was with her therapist, or acupuncturist, or getting a pedicure, or having a deep-tissue massage, or whichever one she goes to today. She called me back when she got home, and when I told her I *had* to talk to her, like any best friend, she was out the door and on her way over before clicking off.

"I can't believe you're going through with this baseball stunt," she said, marching into my room, settling into my desk chair, and taking over my Mac.

"It's not a stunt."

"Whatever you say." She sipped her can of Fresca. "You'll stop at nothing, Miller."

"What's that supposed to mean?" I asked.

"Hon, it means you'll do anything to get into the boys' locker room. Miller, you're dyin' for a look at what you're not getting!" She cracked her gum.

"Shut up, Sam."

"You know I'm right." She cracked her gum again. "You'd do just about anything to get into Brandon's pants."

"Shut up, Sam."

I love my best friend so much.

"So why's Basset letting you play?"

"Why? Well, for one thing, you should've seen Nathalie the other day."

"She put on a show?" Sam spun away from my computer.

"A show? I swear to god, Sam, I thought Big Bad Bill was going to shit his pants."

"Did she bring him to the Advil point?" Sam asked.

"Advil *and* antacid!"

"Damn, Miller." Sam turned back to the computer. "Even I haven't done that yet."

"Yet."

And Sam has come awful close on more than one occasion.

Last semester, for instance, she took Speech and Public Speaking as an elective. One assignment required the students to present a how-to speech. Students chose their own topics, and most went with the mundane, like how to wrap a present, how to change a diaper, or how to prepare a resume. Not Sam. Sam stood in front of the class and delivered an eight-minute exposé on how to roll a cigarette, a presentation that included visual aids such as three types of rolling paper, four strands of tobacco, two lighters—childproof and non-childproof—matches, and a rolling machine.

That's my Sam.

"Miller, you didn't answer my question. Why's Basset letting you play?"

"Let's just say Basset has the wrong impression about something."

"What does he have the wrong impression about?"

"We had a long talk today before practice."

Sam took another sip of soda. "Miller, are you going to play games, or are you going to tell—"

"He thinks I'm a lesbian!"

Fresca shot from Sam's mouth and nose.

"*What?*"

"That's revolting, Sam. Start cleaning."

"I'm not cleaning anything until you tell me why on earth he thinks you're a lesbian." Sam wiped her mouth and made a face at the saliva-soda sprayed all over my Mac. "This is good stuff, Miller. I need all the details."

"He thinks I'm a lesbian because that's what Brandon told him." I grabbed a handful of tissues and began wiping the mess.

"Miller, you need to talk to Brandon. Find out why he said that."

"You think? Oh, thanks for the advice, Sam."

"You're welcome. I'm good with this sort of thing." Sam replaced her gum with a fresh piece. "But I am confused about one thing."

"Sam, you're always confused."

She blew a bubble. "Big Bill Basset is your mom's boyfriend. He's gonna find out you're not gay."

"No, he's not."

"What do you mean he's not? You're really gonna pretend to be a lesbian just to play baseball?"

I nodded.

"Oh, honey." Sam walked over and hugged me. "You are so pathetic. Miller, even for you this reaches new—"

"Get off!" I pushed her away. "I can do this. I know I can. But I need your help."

"You need my help? You're asking me to help you pretend to be a lesbian?"

I nodded again.

"Okay." Sam shrugged. "Sounds like it could be fun."

"You will?"

"Sure, Miller. Why not? As long as we don't have to fool around or anything or pretend to date. If I ever did decide to do lesbo, you'd hardly be my type."

"So you'll help me?" I wasn't quite sure Sam was getting this.

"What did I just say?" Sam had a gleeful grin on her face. "Yes. I'll go along with this. It'll be an adventure. Just tell me what you need me to do, and I'll do it." Sam turned off my computer without powering down. "Now let's go shopping."

"What are you doing? Where are you going?" I sat down on my bed.

"Miller, you said we needed to talk. We talked. You said you needed me to help you be a lesbian. I said okay. Now I need to go shopping. You're not the only one with needs." She glanced at her watch on the way to the door. "Shit! My stores are closing."

"Sucks for you," I said.

"Ice cream!" She raced over, grabbed me by the arm, and dragged me out of my room.

That's my Sam.

I take it you're able to figure that Sam tends to deal with things quite differently than most. I love the girl to death, but with her impulse-driven and addictive personality she does have issues. Mad issues.

Allow me to elaborate:

For one thing, Sam is spoiled rotten. We're talking daddy's-platinum-Visa-and-mommy's-BMW-at-her-disposal spoiled rotten. Now bear in mind, mommy's Beemer is a two-seater, and there are three people in Sam's family. So there shouldn't be any question as to where some of Sam's values and priorities come from.

Sam also loves to collect things. Well, maybe *amass* things is more like it. Like fashion magazines—she's on every direct-mail catalog list known to womankind—and CDs—store-bought, online-purchased, and self-burned—and god knows why, considering the only music she listens to these days is on her iPods. Yes, that's iPods, plural. But who am I to question?

Sam's a partier as well. Not a druggie or an alcoholic partier, but she definitely likes to have a good time. Often. Which as a second-semester senior means five nights a week. Minimum.

On top of all this, Sam is boy-crazy. Now while many girls suffer from this affliction (myself included, despite my sudden lesbianese), Sam, in her usual fashion, takes things to an extreme. Now Sam doesn't sleep around per se; she just likes to fool around. A lot. According to Sam, high school boys *need* to gain sexual experience; otherwise they risk being subjected to endless hours of ridicule, teasing, and torment. I agree completely, but that doesn't mean *she* has to be their practice dummy! Thankfully Sam's always safe about things. She may be somewhat of a ho, but she's not *that* stupid.

Lately, however, I must admit there has been a noticeable change in Sam's boy mania. That's because for the first time since we've been friends, she's started dating someone semi-seriously (translation: more than a month).

The guy is Sam, and he happens to be the second baseman on the varsity baseball team.

Yes, Sam and Sam.

I kid you not. Can you imagine that? I don't know what I would do if I happened to like someone with the same name as me. But I guess at the moment I have other, more pressing concerns to worry about.

"Miller, now that you're on the baseball team, you'd better not try to hit on my boyfriend."

"*Puh-lease.*"

We were in the car on our way to satisfy her ice cream fix, the next best thing after shopping.

"I expect you'll talk me up. Put in a good word."

"Sam, you're going out with the boy. Why do you need me to put in a good word?"

She leaned over and fumbled with the stereo. "Hon, I want to make sure he likes me."

I smacked her hand and pointed her eyes back to the road. "I hope you're kidding."

She curled her lip. "We've only been going out two months."

"He likes you, Sam. Trust me." The car drifted onto the shoulder, so I reached over and helped her align the steering wheel.

As one can easily deduce, Sam's driving skills are another problem area, and riding shotgun with her is not exactly a nerve-easing experience.

"Wait a sec," Sam said. Her brat smile had returned, but I didn't care because she was momentarily watching the road. "Why am I worried about you hitting on my boyfriend? You're a lesbo now. How silly of me. I was right, Miller. This will be fun."

"Very funny, bitch."

"And what does Nathalie think about all this?"

I didn't answer.

"Miller?"

Sam picked her cell phone off the console, but I snatched it from her before she could start downloading ring tones, texting, or doing whatever else she felt compelled to do while operating a motorized vehicle (if you could call what she was doing operating a motorized vehicle).

"Nathalie knows only that I'm allowed to play," I answered. "She doesn't know under what circumstances."

"Really?" Sam grinned mischievously. "The plot thickens."

"Oh, don't look so happy about it, and whatever you do, don't you dare say a word to her."

"Oh, come on, Miller. You know I'd never say anything." Sam was cracking her gum again. "I wouldn't out you to your own mother. What kind of friend do you think I am?" Sam inspected her lipstick in the rearview mirror. "But I have to tell you, I can't wait to tell this to my therapist."

"Excuse me?" I palmed the top of her head and rotated it back toward the road.

"Even before this lesbian thing, my therapist thought you were projecting."

"*What?*" I lowered the volume.

"She says you're attention-deprived, and that you have issues in your life that you refuse to address."

I hit mute. "Sam, why are you talking to your psychologist about me?"

"Psychiatrist," she corrected me. "Do you really think I'd go to a doctor who lacked the power to prescribe?"

"You're worse than my mom. Now don't ignore my question."

"Miller, I talk about you in therapy all the time." Sam turned the music back on. "Why does this come as news?"

"Sam, when you are at therapy, shouldn't you be talking about someone else?" I paused. "Like *you*?"

She curled her lip. "It gets so boring. I hate always talking about me. Sam this, Sam that. Sam, Sam, Sam."

"Your parents are shelling out two hundred bucks an hour." I knew that meant nothing to her.

"My therapist and I enjoy talking about other people." She looked at me and then started to inspect her eyeliner in the rearview mirror. "I think I'd make a good therapist. Maybe that's what I should be, a therapist."

"Sam!" I flung my free arm forward and pointed to the road.

"Miller, relax." Sam swerved the car back into the lane and smiled at me. "That wasn't even close."

My fingernails were digging into the dashboard. Trust me, once you've driven with Sam, you never again take passenger-side airbags for granted.

"You're wack, Sam. You know that?"

"I'm wack? Miller, I'm not the one pretending to be gay." Sam blew a bubble in my direction.

I palmed the top of her head again and rotated it back toward the road. "I didn't choose this."

"Spoken like a true lesbian."

Ever since that song about irony came out all those years ago, I've been a little unclear about the real meaning of the word. But if my understanding is accurate, there is definitely something ironic about having to pretend I'm gay while embroiled in the fight of fights with my only gay friend.

Let me tell you, every teenage girl needs to have a close gay male friend to help her maneuver through the minefield of high school. It should be a requirement like biology or global studies. A close gay male friend provides you with essential and immeasurable insights into the opposite sex, and he provides these essential and immeasurable insights willingly and without the usual ulterior sexual motives.

That's definitely among the things I've missed the most about Josh during our near year of estrangement.

Anyway, the playground around the corner from Josh's house is *our* spot, or at least it used to be. Whenever Josh and I wanted to chill, we would go there. We'd sit on the swings, or on top of the slide, or in the sandbox, or wherever, and just hang. On more than a few occasions, we got pretty shit-faced drinking peach schnapps and hard lemonade, and we got pretty baked there a number of times as well (especially on the choice Thai stick we sometimes managed to get our hands on).

Josh was already sitting on our bench by the basketball court when I arrived.

"Brandon outed me." I cut right to the chase.

"You're late," he replied coldly.

I rolled my eyes. "Brandon outed me," I repeated.

"I heard you the first time. What does *that* mean?"

"Brandon outed me to his father."

"BSB, stop talking in riddles. What does that mean?"

"Well, to tell you the truth, I'm not really sure, but to make a long story short, Principal Basset's letting me play baseball because he thinks I'm a lesbian."

"And you're allowing this to happen?"

I nodded.

"Why didn't you say anything? Why didn't you tell Basset the truth?"

"Because I want to play baseball."

"What does being a lesbian have to do with playing baseball?"

A fair question, and one I still didn't have a very good answer for, although I was somewhat surprised Josh even bothered to ask it considering that as GSA president, Josh also had to endure and accept an endless number of inane decisions on the part of one Principal Basset.

"It's the only way I can play."

"The only way? BSB, if you're gay, I'm straight!" Josh looked away and placed his hands atop his shaking head. "You know how I feel about things like this."

"Here we go. Things? What things, Josh?"

"You're never gonna get it. You still don't have a clue about what it's like—"

"Josh, what are you talking about?"

Phil Bildner

But to tell you the truth, I knew *exactly* what he was talking about. From the moment I knew I was going to have this conversation, I knew this was the direction it was going to take.

"BSB, we don't talk anymore, and *this* is the reason why. You still have no clue how much you hurt me."

"Let's get something perfectly clear, Josh. I'm through arguing with you. It's always the same thing, and we never get anywhere. You know it, and I know it. So what's the point? But for a change, this isn't about you. This is about *me*."

"Bullshit, BSB." Josh stood up and glared. "Of course this is about me."

"No, Josh—"

"No, BSB! You said it yourself in the student lounge this afternoon. You said it involved me, the GSA, and Brandon. Remember?"

Shit, that's *exactly* what I had said.

Suddenly it felt like last year all over again. Josh and I were at each other's throats and fighting about something related to the GSA.

The GSA. The beginning of the end of Darcy and Josh.

When Josh started the GSA, I couldn't have been more proud of him. How could I not be? Here he was building this club as a way to promote tolerance and community. He wanted to educate people and bring people together.

And he did. He succeeded. I was so impressed by his level of commitment, and of course, I backed him one hundred percent, every step of the way.

With Josh leading the way, the GSA created pamphlets and informational flyers. They built a Web site, they sponsored guest speakers, and they actively promoted AIDS Awareness Day and

National Coming Out Day. They got written up (several times) in local newspapers, and they were even featured in a segment on the evening news.

But rather quickly, the GSA started taking precedent over everything. *Everything.* It turned into an all-consuming undertaking. Every day it was another meeting, and more phone calls, and planning this activity, and scheduling that activity, and doing outreach at this school, and . . . and it never stopped. It took over Josh's life.

And I resented that. I admit it. I have no problem admitting it. I resented that our Josh-Darcy time was being victimized by Josh's obsession, which was exactly what the GSA had turned into.

"I can't believe you're actually going through with this." Josh was still shaking his head.

"I want to play baseball," I answered flatly.

"And you have no problem misleading people like this?"

"I'd prefer if I didn't have to, but—"

"But you'll do it if it means you can play baseball."

"You know how much I love baseball. Think about it from my point of view."

"From your point of view? Are you kidding?" Josh forced a laugh. "It's dishonest. You're a liar."

"It's only baseball, Josh."

"No, BSB, this is so much more than baseball."

"Here we go again! Let me guess: This is about *your* sexuality, *your* oppression, right?"

Because that's exactly the pattern that developed last year. Everything always ended up heading down that road, and when it did, I started not only to resent what was happening between Josh and me, but to resent the GSA as well. Let me tell you, that's not a particularly popular opinion to have about a student organization whose primary objectives are to educate and enlighten.

But in my defense, the GSA *had* lost its way. I mean, it was still about tolerance and community, but it became something else. It became this forum for anger and outrage. Every single issue somehow became connected to sexuality and oppression. Every single injustice and anything unfair were suddenly rooted in homophobia, sexual bigotry, and intolerance toward gays.

I had no qualms about saying my mind to Josh. That pissed him off like nobody's business.

And he was nobody's business pissed off right now. Josh was getting increasingly worked up, and I have to admit I was thoroughly enjoying it.

"BSB, the world doesn't see things the way you do."

"What is that supposed to mean?"

"It's your world." Josh shook his head more adamantly than ever. "The rest of us are just passing through. Visitors on a tour."

"You're speaking nonsense."

"How can one person look at the world through such a narrow lens?"

"You know something, Josh? That's the same exact thing you said all last year. I didn't understand it then, and I don't understand it now."

"I wouldn't expect you to."

It still unnerves me to think about how quickly things deteriorated between us last year. The way I saw things, the more out Josh became, the more outspoken, outrageous, outlandish, and out of his freakin' mind he was becoming. But to him, I was increasingly intolerant, narrow-minded, and shortsighted, and because I didn't lockstep agree with *everything* he stood for, I was wrong and right-wing.

Things got so bad that I started doing things to intentionally piss him off. Started pushing all his buttons. Hard. The boy needed to take it down a notch and not just see things in black and white (or straight and gay).

For one thing, I started calling him "NJ" for New Josh, and "OJ" for Old Josh. Trust me, he didn't like that one, especially because it was a backhanded, passive-aggressive way of associating him with an alleged pathological, wife-beating murderer, and because I was also well aware of his thoughts on that proud moment in American pop culture.

Needless to say, that only widened the Josh-Darcy rift and . . .

Suddenly I started to smile. I knew what was about to happen next.

I don't know what it is with me lately, but I've been experiencing this perverse pleasure in watching people get riled up, enraged, and disgusted. First it was Nathalie in Principal Basset's office; then it was Big Bad Bill during our little one-on-one; then it was Irv at practice; and now it was about to be Josh's turn.

But to be perfectly fair, I've always liked watching Josh get flustered and irritated. I swear, if you didn't know him, you'd think he was having a seizure!

When someone gets under his skin, he's quite the entertainment centerpiece. He'll start to flail his arms and hands all about, and he'll twitch his head to the side like a swimmer trying to shake water from his ear. And speaking of ears, when Josh is really juiced, both of his ears turn bright red. Personally, I think it's adorable, but he hates it. Hates it! He can feel it when it starts to happen, so he'll cover his ears with his hands. Now think about this for a second: When you're engaged in a heated debate or discussion, arguing with your hands over your ears simply doesn't cut it. People think he's being rude and childish when he's merely hiding an insecurity and vulnerability.

Phil Bildner

And that didn't used to be the worst of it. During these frustration fits, Josh used to also get these snot bubbles that would just sit on the end of his nostrils. Thankfully, he's learned to control that disability.

Longdeeplongdeeplongdeep breath.

Now was as good a time as any (maybe the perfect time) to let the other shoe drop.

"Josh, there's more."

No response.

"Josh, there's more."

"More what?"

"More. More to this baseball-lesbian thing."

He just glared.

Longdeeplongdeeplongdeep breath.

"Basset's making me join GSA."

"Oh no, he's not."

I nodded.

"No fuckin' way!"

"He's making Brandon join too."

"No fuckin' way!"

"We'll both be at the meeting day after tomorrow."

"BSB, there's no way in hell you're joining GSA."

"Well, Josh, I really don't think that's up to you."

"You're such a hypocrite. All you ever did was bad-mouth the GSA."

"No, I didn't."

"You said we were a bunch of fanatics. Zealots."

I guess I did say that, too. Josh can be quite skilled at turning my own words against me. I hate that.

"We're forcing the issue on people," he continued. "Shoving it down their throats, remember?"

"You're right, Josh. I did say that. But I didn't say it about everything."

Josh took a few short breaths, folded his arms, and lowered his head.

Oh shit, now I was doomed.

Not only is Josh skilled at turning my own words against me, but he also knows how to push *my* buttons, make me feel bad no matter how pissed I am. All he needs to do is relax his face, take a few short breaths, fold his arms, lower his head, and then peer up at me with those puppy-dog eyes.

Like now.

"BSB," he said, his tone softer, "when I used to tell you I hated being teased, you used to say everyone gets teased."

"Everyone does."

"Fine. Everyone does. But not everyone gets called 'butt-pirate.'" Josh stepped closer. "Not everyone gets called 'fudge packer.'"

"Everyone gets teased, Josh. It doesn't matter if you're gay, straight, or whatever."

"That's right, BSB." Josh was getting emotional. I hated it when he got emotional. Because I turned even softer. "Don't you dare try to tell me those words should empower me. Don't you dare try to tell me those words should make me stronger. Those words hurt."

I wasn't quite sure why he was telling me this right now, but I immediately flashed back to the speech he gave at freshman orientation last year. While all the clubs, groups, organizations, and teams "sales pitched" the ninth graders, Josh used the GSA's three-minute allotment to open eyes and ears.

"Society has evolved, except in its attitude toward gays," he had said. "Yeah, we have become much more tolerant, but gays are still

Phil Bildner

fair game. To be gay is still going against the grain. It's still swimming upstream."

He had hopped off the auditorium stage and walked right up to the newest members of the Finley student body.

"Cognizance," he spoke loudly and without a microphone. "That's the word I want you to remember: cognizance. It's an awareness, a constant consciousness. When you're gay, you have this awareness of every comment, whistle, whisper, and elbow. Cognizance. You know it's directed at you, and you know why it's directed at you. Every push, shove, and punch. Cognizance."

And then he gave those examples:

"When you're gay, you're target practice during dodgeball, but you don't get pegged by the red rubber balls or Nerf balls. You get drilled by the errant, overinflated basketball.

"When you're gay, your car always gets boxed in. And whenever another car has its windows broken or tires slashed, you can guarantee it will happen to yours, too. It won't happen to yours by itself because then people will know, and people can't know. But *you* know. These aren't random acts. No, these are hardly random acts of violence."

I turned back to Josh. Somehow we had made our way across the playground, and he had walked up the slide.

He was sitting in the spot, the exact spot where he had been when he reached into his pocket and read me that poem. The poem that I still keep in my jewelry box. The poem that I know by heart.

How Many Ways
How many ways
How many ways can I put this

Can't stick it in a drawer
Hide it behind my socks or 'neath my sweaters or next to
*   where I keep my cash*

Ain't no on/off switch
Can't click it like the lights or the TV or the ringer on the phone

It's in my bed at night
When I stare at the ceiling with my hands clasped behind my head and
*   when I turn over and when I bury my head under my pillows and when*
*   I hide 'neath my comforter*

This ain't no game of hide 'n' seek either
Can't run away or duck behind the bushes or slip under a car or get lost
*   in a crowd*

No vacation
Not from this
A few days in the country or a plane ride someplace warm
This comes along for the trip

I have no say in the matter
It appears when it wants to appear
Like it has a mind of its own
Which it does

So
How many ways
How many ways can I put this?

That's simple
When I breathe, it breathes

I stood at the bottom of the ramp and looked up to him. "Actually Josh, you should be glad Basset's making us join. It'll be good for GSA."

"You're not funny."

"I'm not trying to be. I'm serious."

"It's *my* club, BSB. *My* club!" Josh's tone was finding its edge again. "I won't allow this. I'll expose you both."

Phil Bildner

"Expose us? What would you do that for? You're finally getting the chance to be near your dream boy. You've always had the biggest schoolgirl crush on Brandon. Maybe this is your chance to convert—"

"BSB, this isn't funny. I'm being serious."

"Too serious, if you ask me."

"Well, no one's asking you."

"That's right, Josh. You wouldn't *ever* ask me." I couldn't hold back. "You might have to hear something you don't want to."

"Shut up, BSB. You're not getting away with any of this. Not while I'm president."

"I'm telling you, Josh, this isn't up to you."

"It's bad enough people still don't take GSA seriously. It's bad enough we have teachers and administrators at Finley who still snicker at us behind our backs."

"What's your point?"

"It's bad enough people think we're already on our last leg. There's no *way* you two will make a mockery of us. No way." He headed off.

"Josh, we're not finished talking about this."

"Oh, I'm finished. And if you show up at GSA with Brandon, you're finished too." He kicked sand in my direction. "BSB, there's no way you're getting away with this lying-lesbian shit! No way in hell! If you think we were at war before this, think again. You should've known better than to mess with me."

12

Not surprisingly, I didn't sleep a wink, so on top of being as nervous as a Jehovah's Witness with a severed artery, I was also thoroughly exhausted as I headed out to my first practice the following day.

I had no idea what Brandon had told his (our) teammates, but based on the sideways glances, the questioning looks, and the eerie silence, I knew that "Darcy the lesbian" was out and about.

I stretched by myself on the grass by the bleachers.

I just want to play for the baseball team. Take the field. Hear my name announced. "Now batting: Darcy Miller."

That's what I kept telling myself. I'd be able to handle all the bullshit if I could keep my focus.

Still, it was gnawing at me that I had not yet been able to confront Brandon. I thought about doing it here at practice, but that would cause a major and most unnecessary scene, and the last thing I needed was to give my teammates yet another reason to hate my guts and despise my presence, especially because, on my way from the lockers, I had learned of another reason why they could.

Up until the day before, the team hadn't practiced with bats and balls. For the first week and a half of practice, the team only did player-led conditioning sessions—wind sprints, suicides, distance running, slide-stepping drills. Seventy-five minutes each day. Irv believes this approach builds camaraderie, but everyone dreaded these first six afternoons because they were absolutely brutal.

So for me to just show up for my tryout on day seven . . .

Irv blew his whistle and gathered the team at home plate.

"When you're on my field, you're on my field one hundred percent." Irv wasted no time getting down to business. "I have you ninety minutes an afternoon, and for those ninety minutes, you're mine."

Irv runs a tight, no-nonsense ship. I love that. I believe a good high school coach must conduct organized sessions with clear and stringent expectations.

Irv's practices emphasized fundamentals and situations, and to accomplish this he used rotating stations at fifteen-minute intervals. But at the beginning of preseason, all pitchers and catchers were exempted from station work in order to work separately with Bro. Bro insisted on this because varsity and junior varsity determinations were yet to be made, and he liked to get a look at the crop of arms coming down the road.

So I was instructed to go with Bro and the rest of the pitchers and catchers to the utility mounds in the end zone of the football field where the track team was practicing.

"Yo, who's catchin' the dyke?"

The first words I heard within five seconds of reaching the mounds.

Under normal circumstances I would have pounced, but these were anything but normal circumstances. It was a given that I was going to be tested, and I needed to keep my composure.

I turned in the direction of the question. Three freshmen looked at each other with "not me" expressions, but I knew in an instant it was the Ignorant Crack Baby Moron in the middle.

Ignorant Crack Baby Moron—I can't actually take credit for coming up with the nickname on a moment's notice. It was a mnemonic device I used in American History last year. We were studying the cold war, and I couldn't keep track of all the different types of arms-race missiles, so I thought up these ridiculous acronyms, and Ignorant Crack Baby Moron was the one for ICBM, intercontinental ballistic missile. With memory devices like that, you never forget anything!

I stepped toward the three without saying a word. I needed to keep my cool, but I also needed to show I wasn't about to be trampled upon at will.

"Yo, your field's over there." Ignorant Crack Baby Moron lifted his catcher's mask onto his head and pointed toward the softball practice. "What are you trying to prove by playin' baseball anyways?"

I stepped closer. I could feel myself starting to tremble. Not a good sign. I pointed at him. "Catch me."

"Yo, I ain't catchin' no dyke."

"What'd you say?" I could no longer hold back.

"Get out of my face, Lezzie."

"The word is lesbian." I grabbed his mask and pulled it back down over his face. "And it's not a slur, so don't use it as one."

"Don't touch, bitch!"

I pulled his face close. "Listen, Ignorant Crack Baby Moron, don't you ever speak to, at, or about me like that again." I snapped his mask into his face. "The word is lesbian. It's who I am. Deal with it."

So much for keeping cool and maintaining my composure.

"Whoa, Lassie!" Bro charged over and stepped between us. "There a probl'm here?"

"Not with me," I replied, breathing hard and staring down Ignorant Crack Baby Moron.

Bro turned to the catcher, whose entire clenched face was quivering. "Well, son, I reckon, you squat and take Lassie's pitches, if you can handle 'em."

You tell him, Bro!

"I doubt he'll be able to," I mumbled under my breath.

ICBM whirled back. "What'd you just say?" He stepped toward me, pointing.

"Whoa!" Bro held out his arms like he was separating sparring boxers. "That's it! I ain't gonner have this type o' nonsense on my mounds. Now let's get to work here."

After one final stare-down, I headed to the mound. But I was rattled. Ignorant Crack Baby Moron had gotten to me.

Suddenly I felt myself free-falling into an all-out anxiety attack, a truly special genetic hand-me-down Nathalie has gifted me, and one that, despite what she claims, no amount of Dr. St. Claire rhythmic breathing can fully ward off. I had never experienced anything remotely like this on a field. The baseball diamond was Darcy Miller's "happy place," not a setting for a full-force frontal freak-out!

I needed to do something quick.

I needed to pitch.

13

"So how many pitches you throw, Lassie?" Bro asked.

"Three or four."

"Well, Lassie, which is it? Three or four?"

"I'd probably only throw three in a game." I stepped onto the mound and kicked around some dirt.

"Then I reckon you got three pitches. What's that there fourth pitch you don't throw?"

"A curveball."

"No Uncle Charlie? Shucks, I reckon all my pitchers throw breakin' balls."

I took a long breath. For a moment, I thought I was going to have to disclose Miller family skeletons and explain why I didn't throw a curveball, but Irv took me off the hook (so to speak).

He placed a ball in my glove. "I gotta tell you, Lassie, if you don't throw no hook, you're gonna need to sell me."

Sell you? *Puh-lease.*

"Bro, I've got three pitches." I dropped my glove to the pitching rubber and gripped the ball. "I throw my fastball cross-seam because I get better movement than if I throw it with the seams." I held the grip out for inspection. "On *my* fastball, movement is much more important than velocity."

"Wish all my pitchers believed that. Reckon everyone here be too concerned with overpowerin' everyone."

"Well, Bro, I'm not exactly gonna overpower anyone." I changed my grip and held it out again. "I also throw a splitter, but I throw that with the seams. I don't spread my fingers too far apart, so I ain't gonner blow out my elbow."

Ain't gonner blow out my elbow? Good god! Bro's drawl was contagious!

I showed him one more grip. "My best pitch is my change."

"Your change-up's yer out pitch?" Bro asked, surprised. He scratched his head.

"My arm speed doesn't change whatsoever. Plus I hold the ball back in my hand, and I vary the placement ever so slightly." I held out my hand palm up. "That allows me to mix speeds on my change."

"Reckon I'll have to see that. Where'd you learn all this, Lassie?"

"Just know it."

"Brother?"

"Nope."

"Father?"

I froze. Did I really have to go here? I thought I had already dodged this bullet.

My dad is the reason I love baseball. He's also the reason I'm so good at it. I may hate the man for abandoning Nathalie and me, but I am gifted with his ball-playing abilities. I guess that makes baseball genetic—unlike lesbianism, which as you now know is purely one's choice.

My dad would've played professional ball. That's what everyone always told me. That is, if he hadn't blown out his elbow in college. Which is why he never let me throw a curve. He taught me every other pitch, and he even showed me a curveball grip, but he never wanted to see what happened to him happen to his little girl.

Such a considerate man.

I took another long breath and shook my head. "My dad taught me baseball, but before you start asking anything else, the bastard's been MIA since middle school. Closest thing I have to a father nowadays is . . ."

I stopped. I couldn't believe *that* entered my head *and* left my lips. I shuddered. Talk about places I didn't want to go!

"Let's see what you got." Bro stepped to the side of the mound and pointed Ignorant Crack Baby Moron into his crouch. "Whenever you're ready, Lassie."

Oh, I was ready. And I was butter!

I threw twenty-three pitches. And with each pitch, Bro's expression of pleasure, delight, satisfaction, and sheer bliss grew and grew.

Bro had his ace.

But I have to tell you: As I was pitching, something weird was happening. I couldn't stop thinking about Brandon. *Brandon.* I even turned to look for him. Twice! And when I didn't spot him on the field with the rest of the team, it bothered me. *Annoyed* me. And then when I finally did spot him behind the backstop with the hitting group, this wave of relief rushed over me—like the feeling you get when you're keeping tabs on someone.

I had no idea what to make of these sabotaging thoughts, but I knew it couldn't be good.

"I reckon I'm gonna say this straight out, Lassie, so you know exactly where I stand in all this." Bro was alongside me on the mound motioning toward where the remainder of the team was practicing. "When we head on back over, and Irv there asks me for my

Phil Bildner

impressions, I reckon I'm gonna tell him I gots me a new number one starter."

I was beaming. How could I not be?

"I'm gonna tell him my new ace is me Lassie. 'Course he's gonner have to see for himself, and he's gonner wanna see what else you can do, but I reckon I don't got me another pitcher on this here staff who mixes speeds quite like you do. Yer gonna drive them hitters nuts!"

I turned around and looked back at Steven Phillips, aka "Specs" because of his ridiculous Coke-bottle glasses, and Reynaldo Lopez, the team's only left-handed pitcher. Last year, they had been the team's number one and number two starters, respectively. They had both watched and witnessed my dazzling spectacle and display, and I guess because of the ICBM incident, I was fearing the worst. But they seemed to be okay with all this. In fact, they appeared genuinely pumped.

"Way to throw." Specs walked right up to me and high-fived my glove.

"Thanks."

"You throw like that when it counts, and we'll win this thing going away," Reynaldo added.

"Thanks."

"Don't worry about him." Specs motioned in the direction of ICBM. "He's a prick."

"Thanks."

"Yeah, next time he says something," Reynaldo took the ball from my glove and pounded it into his. "Let me know. I'll take care of it."

"Thanks."

Bro draped an arm around me. "Reckon I'm thinkin' 'bout

tinkerin' with your mechanics a lit'le. Might be able to get a li'l more pop out of your fastball, but I doubt if it's even necessary. Sound all right by you, Lassie?"

"Thanks."

"No, thank you, Lassie. Reckon I'm glad you had the balls . . . I mean . . . I mean . . . I'm glad you had the guts to join this here squad. Thinks you might be our missin' piece."

"*Think?* What do you mean *think?*"

I was floating. Float-ting.

Thinks you might be our missin' piece.

I didn't need to be the missing piece. I mean it felt great to be thought of that way, but I was satisfied with just taking the field.

I was floating. Float-ting.

Heading back to my car after that first practice, nothing could bring me down from . . .

Josh.

Nothing could bring me down from the rush I was experiencing except for Josh, who was leaning against the driver's-side door of my car.

"Move," I said.

He didn't budge.

"I said move."

For two people who were supposedly on nonspeaking terms, we sure were doing our fair share of interacting, and his presence at this moment couldn't be good.

"What flavor are you?" he asked.

"What?"

"I asked what flavor are you?"

"What?"

"Lesbian, BSB. What flavor *lesbian* are you?"

I knew exactly what he was talking about. I had heard Josh's flavor tirade several times before, so rather than fight what I knew was coming, I allowed him to roll into his little rant.

"On the rare occasion Finley kids allow themselves to think about lesbians, they get these stereotypical ideas in their pea brains. Of course, there's the lipstick lesbian. She struts the halls Revloned to the max, wearing her hiked-up Dolce or Prada, taunting, goading, and tempting the chanceless male population. Then there's the motorcycle-woodshop lesbian. The whole dykes-on-bikes thing. That's the girl with the cropped hair, the leather jacket, and the monkey wrench in the back pocket of her tattered denim jeans. Then you got the WNBA-wannabe lesbian. She spends her time with the gym rats showing off her basketball skills. She wears oversized hoodies and ridiculously baggy jeans. Finally, you have the piece-of-art lesbian. She's pierced her ears, nose, chin, navel, and a few other body parts that make you cringe at the mere thought. She's also a walking tattoo—forearms, back of the neck, inner thigh, and all the usual locales."

"You finished?"

"Which flavor are you?"

He didn't give me time to answer (not that I would have).

"I've been thinking about yesterday." Josh still blocked the door. "I'm willing to make a deal."

"I'm not interested in any of your deals," I lied. "Move!"

"It's in your best interest to listen."

Josh had succeeded in ruining my natural high, and right now I so wanted to shove him aside and throw him to the pavement, but resorting to bodily harm was an option I could ill afford. If Lucifer was offering *any* type of deal, I needed to hear him out.

But I wasn't quite ready. Not just yet.

"You had something to do with what happened at practice today, didn't you?" I stepped too close. "You put that freshman up to it. What did you do? Pay him off?"

"Cut your lame games." Josh wasn't having it. "You know I had nothing to do with whatever happened at practice."

Of course I knew he had nothing to do with the ICBM incident.

"But if something did happen," Josh continued, "I'm glad. It's exactly why I'm allowing you to go through with this baseball thing."

"Allowing me? You're *allowing* me to go through with this? *Puh-lease*, Josh. How many times do I have to tell you it's not up to you?"

"No, BSB, it *is* up to me. *I'm* allowing it." He paused. "But only for a little while."

"A little while? What does that mean?"

"It means what it means."

Not the answer I was looking for. What was he going to do? Let me play for a few days or a couple weeks and then blow my cover?

"BSB, you're about to learn some harsh lessons. Kids at Finley—kids in general—are ignorant. You never believed it, no matter what you may say, but now you're going to see for yourself. I don't know if you can handle it like I can."

"Oh, I love it when you act all butch, Josh."

"Maybe this lesbian thing will be good for you after all." Josh hopped onto the hood of my car. "Maybe you'll finally see the light. Get you to finally see just how narrowminded people at this place can be. And get you to finally see just how wrong you've been."

"I'll be okay. Don't worry about it."

But Josh was shaking his head. "This is exactly what you don't understand. This is exactly what you don't respect. You haven't a clue what you're in for, but if this is what it's going to take, then I'm all for it."

"So now you *want* me to play baseball under this false pretense? Even though it's so misleading?"

"No, I want you to get a taste of what it's like for me, even though you can never really know." Josh was off the hood and in front of my car door again. "You're going to come crawling back to me apologizing for being such a BSB."

I rolled my eyes. "Yeah, that's exactly what I'll do."

"Tell me something. What's Samantha's role in all this? I know she's in on this. It reeks of her."

"As a matter of fact, she has nothing to do with any of this."

"But she knows," Josh said, more as a statement than a question.

I didn't answer, and I knew my silence enraged him.

You see, when it comes to Samantha, Josh turns into a fourth grader. That's because Josh and Sam don't like each other. No, I mean, *really* don't like each other! When they talk about the other—or god forbid, when they interact—they get downright evil.

But the funny (or sad) thing is that their mutual hatred makes absolutely no sense because they're a perfect match. They have so much in common. For instance, Josh rivals (and maybe even surpasses) Samantha in the spoiled department. He also has as good (if not better) fashion sense. And in the shoe department, forget it. Josh has her beat hands down several times over, and let me tell you, when a seventeen-year-old fashionista such as Sam is unable to compete with her archnemesis in the footwear department, it's borderline apocalyptic and cataclysmic.

Of course, it almost goes without saying that Sam played a

significant role in the termination of Josh and Darcy relations. She couldn't stand listening to me talk about the problems Josh and I were having, so like the true friend she is, she forced me to choose.

I could be friends with her or friends with Josh. Not both. *She* couldn't take it.

So like any teenager given an ultimatum, I acted out. Sam and I had a huge fight, and I chose to be friends with Josh.

Unfortunately, that didn't go over too well with Josh. He refused to allow Sam to dictate the terms of his and my friendship. Does that make any sense? Don't worry, for a while I didn't have any clue either. In any event, all this marked the start of my "BSB" tag and the severing of ties.

"BSB, Samantha is pathetic. Absolutely pathetic." Josh was now back on my hood and curling his lip in a way disturbingly similar to Sam. "That poster child for legalized abortion's got you so wrapped."

"Josh, Sam has nothing to do with this."

"I know how that bitch-girl operates."

"I'm telling you. She has *nothing* to do with this."

"I'll bet any amount of money, any amount, that she's already begging you to put in a good word with her Sam."

On top of everything else, Josh also happens to be one of those frighteningly perceptive kids who's too smart for his own good.

"I bet she's freaking out 'cause she thinks you might make the moves on her man, right?"

"Not bad," I conceded meekly. I boldly hopped onto the hood next to him.

"Don't get too close."

"If we were still best friends, you would've been proud of me these last coupla days. When I was meeting with Basset, he couldn't get himself to say the words 'gay' or 'lesbian,' so I used your line about them not being slurs. I used it on this freshman at practice also."

"I see what you're trying to do. It's not working."

"Whatever, Josh. I'm just telling you what happened. I thought you would've wanted to hear this."

I know he did.

No matter how much we still "hated" each other, sometimes we momentarily ignored our ongoing feud—but only until one of us said the slightest thing out of line, and then it was back to the fight.

"What did Basset say when you said they weren't slurs?"

I laughed. "Let's just say he wasn't very comfortable with the whole conversation."

Josh allowed himself a soft laugh too. "I can't believe you're getting to . . . I can't believe I'm actually allowing you to play ball with Brandon."

"Jealous?"

"I demand details, specifics, and daily updates."

I grinned.

It felt so good to be talking with Josh again and I know he had to be feeling the same way. He had to be as conflicted—pardon the Dr. St. Claire hand-me-down psychobabble terminology—as I was.

"Before you get any updates, I still need to have quite the talk with that pretty boy."

Josh smacked me on the side of my head. "Don't you *ever* do that!"

"Ow! Do what?"

"That!" He smacked me again and pointed.

"What? Ow!"

"It's all over your face. What you're thinking. Don't you dare go there!"

"Go where?"

"Don't play me!"

Good god! Did being gay also give you ESP?

Whenever I think about a guy *that way*—even the slightest bit—Josh knows it. And he especially knows it when we're attracted to the same guy.

"Let me tell you something, BSB." Josh was off the hood and standing in front of me. "What I said applies to you, not Brandon."

"What applies to me?"

"I'm letting *you* go ahead with this charade, not Brandon. But I'm not just letting you. There are conditions."

Those warm, flashback feelings of friendship had vanished as quickly as they had appeared.

"For one thing"—Josh was pointing—"you two show up at GSA tomorrow, and you've both had it."

"Josh, why all of a sudden—"

"Shut up! *You* can play baseball. *You* can go to GSA, but not *him*. I'm teaching *you* the lesson, BSB."

Like someone with a split personality, Josh was back into bitch-overdrive. Perhaps "conflicted" was the correct terminology after all.

"So then what happens if—"

"Shut up!" Josh was in full-fluster mode, with arms and hands flailing, head twitching, ears reddening, and the makings of a throwback snot bubble growing on his nostril. "You do it *my* way, BSB, and if you choose not to, not only do *you* lose, but I'll bring *everyone* down."

Horrific visions flashed before my eyes.

If Josh wanted to, if he truly wanted to, he could do serious damage. Josh knew the truth about so much. Too much. He could expose everything down to the fact that daddy-principal was a puppet controlled by son-student. That was the type of dish-out dirt that could mess with tenure or admittance into coveted assisted-living facilities in South Florida.

"See this?" Josh reached into his back pocket, pulled out a piece of paper, and shoved it in my face. "See it?"

I swallowed hard.

"BSB, this is phase one!"

I was staring at a picture of me planting an openmouthed, protruding-tongue, lip-to-lip kiss on Juan Reyes, Finley's very own senior supermodel, who had his own underwear contract and did television commercials for alkaline batteries. Sure I could easily explain the photograph. *Everybody* wanted to kiss Juan Reyes, whether gay, straight, or celibate. The problem was the caption Josh had superimposed across the image: "Gay? Darcy Miller? Judge for yourself at GSA."

"Phase one, BSB. Phase one!" Josh was still in maximum fluster mode. "I swear to god, no way are you gonna turn gay life, *my* life, into a circus sideshow. I'll make you wish you never wanted to flirt with baseball. Your remaining days at Finley—yours, Brandon's, and anyone else's associated with your little scheme—will be a living hell!"

Not surprisingly, I didn't sleep a wink (again).

Josh had me freaked. How could I not be? He was threatening to out me, bring down the baseball team, *and* destroy my principal, my mother's love interest (ugh!).

Brandon didn't help my sleep either. The longer I went without talking to the boy, the more enraged I became. For sanity's sake, I needed to track him down, and it was getting to the point that I didn't even care if it happened at GSA (well, maybe things hadn't exactly progressed that far).

Thankfully, I spotted him as I passed by the student lounge en route to the GSA. He was sitting in *his* corner, atop the tiered modular furniture (which also happened to be—not accidentally—the farthest point from *my* spot in the lounge).

I snuck up behind him. I needed to catch him off guard.

"Brandon."

He turned around, and his face went full Casper just like his daddy's had two days earlier.

"Hey, Darcy."

"We need to have a talk."

"Look, I'm meeting some of my . . . some of my friends here before . . . before the GSA meeting."

"This'll only take a minute," I replied.

"Darcy, I really want to but—"

I didn't let him finish. I grabbed him by the ear, and lucky for him he didn't pull away, because I wasn't letting go. One long tug and a half dozen steps later, we were out the side entrance to the lounge, and I was kicking open the boys' bathroom door.

"All right," I announced, "everybody out!" I let go of Brandon, but strategically placed myself between him and the exit.

"Jeez, Darcy." Brandon grabbed his ear with both hands and feigned injury.

I looked around the boys' bathroom. Three freshmen. One was at a urinal leaning so far into the porcelain it looked like he was humping the wall, and the other two were stationed in front of the mirror, one engaged in a futile blackhead attack and the other puckering up for some cherry-flavored lip therapy.

Damn! In the boys' bathroom less than five seconds and already provided with enough I-know-stuff-about-you-that-you-don't-want-anyone-ever-to-know ammunition to permanently damage three reputations. Talk about power!

"You really think you should be in here?" Brandon asked. He was still rubbing his ear and trying to be cute about it.

"What difference does it make, Brandon? I'm a lesbian, right?"

With those words, the two freshmen who had been making their way to the door stopped, but I pointed them back toward the exit.

"And don't let anyone else in, zitboys!" I barked.

They nodded obediently and left.

Brandon was smirking.

"You think this is funny?" I stepped toward him.

"Kinda," he shrugged.

"So why'd you say that about me?"

"Say what?"

"That I'm a lesbian."

The boy by the urinal flushed and headed for the sinks, but I pointed him to the door.

"And make sure Fred and Barney are still standing post," I added.

He nodded meekly and walked quickly toward the exit.

"If anything, you should be thanking me." Brandon headed over to the mirrors.

God, he was so cocky. And cute.

"I'm waiting," he said.

"Waiting for what?"

"For you to thank me."

"To thank you?" I laughed. "Thank you for *what*?"

"If it wasn't for me, you wouldn't be playing baseball."

"You've got to be kidding! And what exactly did you tell Bill . . . I mean, Principal Basset . . . I mean, your daddy?"

"It was pretty ingenious of me," Brandon said.

"If you say so yourself."

"Darcy, sexuality is a hot-button issue for my dad. I know how much difficulty he has dealing with it, so I told him since you might be lesbian and since—"

"Might?"

"Uh-huh, might." Brandon tilted his head. "I didn't want to tell a complete untruth, so by saying 'might,' I preserved my out."

"You know I'm not a lesbian. You and I have—"

"You and I have what, Darcy?" Brandon was smirking again. "I don't know *anything* for certain. Anything's possible. We're teenagers. Don't you listen in health class? Adolescence is a period of self-discovery for—"

"*Puh-lease*, Brandon."

"No, Darcy. It's true. We're only learning about ourselves as sexual beings. Anything is possible. That's why I said 'might.' You *might* be a lesbian. I wasn't a hundred percent certain, but I told him to let you play because I didn't want him to have to deal with an uproar."

"You've got to be kidding."

"Not at all."

"That's what scares me."

"Let me ask you something, Darcy: Who do you go out with?"

I wanted to go out with you, dammit!

I could feel the heat building in my cheeks. I didn't like where he was going with this, even though I didn't actually know where that was.

"Who do you?"

Did I just say that? Out loud? How lame!

"Not that it bears any relevance to the situation, but I've dated quite a few Finley girls. But we're talking about you, Darcy. Who have you dated? Guys, not girls."

"Very funny."

Brandon grinned. "Seriously, who've you gone out with?"

"J. D. Black."

"J. D. Black?" He laughed in my face. Literally laughed in my face. "You've got to be kidding! When did you go out with him?"

"Like . . . like we went out for like . . . two months when we were freshmen." I stepped back. Even I couldn't fight off my smile.

Brandon laughed again. He turned on the faucet.

His smugness was driving me crazy! He was toying with me, like he always did whenever no one was around. This was part of his payback for my no-fly zone, and right now I had limited artillery to fire back with.

God, why did he have to be so adorable?

"Darcy, you've had no public heterosexual relationships at Finley. It's one of the main reasons I was able to tell my dad what I did."

"So now I have to go around pretending to be a lesbian?"

"What's the big deal?"

"What's the big deal?" I looked at him in the mirror. "How would you like to have to pretend to be gay?"

"C'mon, Darcy, I could never pull it off. People know I'm straight."

"Well, Brandon," I duh-voiced, "if you started holding hands in the halls with some of your pretty-boy friends, and if you—"

"Nope. Not even then." He smiled as he examined himself in the mirror. "No way could I be a 'mo."

"A 'mo?"

"Yeah. A 'mo. A homo. Gay." He adjusted his perfectly molded, backward baseball cap.

"Brandon, I'm going to have to deal with this twenty-four seven. Peeps are going to be relentless."

Brandon shrugged. "Tell them it's none of their business."

"You think it's going to be that simple?"

"Haven't given it that much thought."

"Obviously."

I was losing this conversation. Badly. Brandon had answers and comebacks for everything, and his nonchalant attitude (not to mention his disarming smile) was nudging me to the brink. I needed to return fire.

"Now that I'm on the team, maybe I should expose your dad's bigoted thinking. Wouldn't that be something a couple months from retirement?"

"What would be the purpose of that? And my dad's not a bigot."

"No? *Puh-lease*, Brandon. I'm a lesbian, and suddenly I'm eligible for boys' baseball? What is that? He can't even get himself to say the words 'gay' and 'lesbian.'"

"My dad's not a bigot," Brandon repeated sternly.

"Trying to convince yourself, Brandon?"

"Listen, Darcy, he may not be the most enlightened individual in the world, but he's not a bigot."

"Oh, that makes a lot of sense." I was loving the sudden shift in balance. "Almost as much sense as my being a lesbian suddenly qualifying me for the boys' baseball team. Being a lesbian shouldn't have made any difference at all."

"Of course it should have. It makes a huge difference, especially with my dad." Brandon's cocky smile reappeared as he shook his head. "Listen, when it comes to issues of sexuality, my dad isn't at his best. I'll admit that."

"That's so big of you."

"In fact, sometimes he thinks irrationally."

"Sometimes?"

"Look, I know my dad's weaknesses. He's a school administrator, and he thinks like one. Rational decision-making and the ability to establish sane policies are not job requirements. You go to high school. You know that." Brandon tapped his chest. "So that's where I come into play. I know how my dad is with controversy—"

"And it's not controversial letting a girl play boys' baseball?"

"It is. But if you look at the big picture, it's not nearly as controversial as excluding a capable girl. If he was to exclude you, Darcy, and you turned out to be better than almost every guy on the team, and the reason why he excluded you was gender-based, that would be flat-out discrimination. That's playing with fire. By letting you play, he is playing with fire. I admit that. But at least that fire is contained."

It was infuriating me how much sense he was making. Brandon knew it too.

It was also infuriating me that he looked so hot while making so much sense. Brandon knew that, too.

"All I did was explain all this to my dad. Spelled it out for him. Showed him both sides, and once I did that, I knew he'd take my advice. He respects me on things like this. I'm very connected to today's youth."

Oh, puke.

But Brandon was serious. That's what frightened me. Well, more like frightened *and* pissed the shit out of me. Brandon had *this* much influence over school policy?

I visibly shuddered.

"Listen, Darcy, your mom never gave my dad—"

"No!" I snapped. "Don't go there! Don't bring my mom into this!" I was yelling. "This has nothing to do with their twisted relationship!"

"Twisted?" Brandon smiled curiously. "I don't think it's twisted at all."

"Of course you wouldn't."

"Personally, I think your mom's mad cool. I think—"

"Personally, I don't want you talking or even thinking about my mom."

Brandon tilted his head puppy-dog cute and shrugged. "Anyway, I knew if I told my dad you were a lesbian—"

"I know why you want me on the team," I interrupted again. "You think I'm that good, don't you? You just want to win, and you know having me on the team is your best chance."

Brandon hopped onto the sink.

"You told your dad we'd win the championship if I was on the team, didn't you?"

Brandon didn't respond.

"Brandon?"

I was on to something. I was going to make him answer.

"Brandon?"

"Yeah, Darcy. I think you're that good."

"I knew it!" I pumped my fist. I *loved* being right. "But Brandon, softball's a different animal than baseball," I added sarcastically. "Ask your daddy."

"I saw you play at the Heatherwood tournament. Anyone with your ability—"

"Heatherwood? That was two years ago."

"And from what I've heard, you're ten times better now."

"And you just assumed I'd go along with your little charade? Ever think that's not what *I* want?"

"I know how badly you want to play baseball."

"Not that badly, Brandon."

"According to my dad, your mom was pretty—"

"According to your dad? Isn't there some kind of ethical conflict with your daddy disclosing things to you?"

Brandon turned on the water and splashed me.

"Hey!" I jumped back. "Don't be an ass!"

"Don't be an ass!" He giggled like a ten-year-old. He hopped down from the sink, tried to splash me again, and then finally stopped. "Look, Darcy, you think you can bring us the championship, and you're probably right."

"No, Brandon, that's what *you* think. Not what *I* think. That's what *you* told your daddy." I placed my hands on my hips and stared. "All that did was confirm what Nathalie had said in his office. It's not what I said."

Brandon paused. "Believe it or not, I think what you just said actually made sense. Not bad. Pretty accurate assessment of the situation. I'm impressed."

"Oh, so now you're going with flattery?"

"Flattery? *Puh-lease*," Brandon mocked me. "Look, Darcy, you don't care about what people think. I know that. You're open-minded when it comes to things. Sexuality, anything. You have to be, considering how close you are with Josh, and everybody knows—"

"Don't say anything bad about Josh."

"Lighten up, Darcy! Jesus! All I was gonna say was everybody knows he's gay."

"Gee, Brandon, it's not like he tries to hide it. He's president of the GSA."

"And he's also been my very own personal stalker since tenth grade!"

I busted out laughing. "I've told you he thinks you don't even know he exists."

"How could I *not* know he exists? Everywhere I turn, I see the kid. He's not dangerous, is he?"

"Until now, no. But you've managed to change that. Trust me."

Brandon Basset is as straight as they come, but that hasn't deterred Josh from engaging in a tireless pursuit of his boy idol, which depending on how you view things has been either impressive or tragic. Josh loses all semblance of sanity when it comes to matters involving Brandon (among other things), and ever since Josh "officially" came out, he has had a major league crush on Brandon, which at times has turned Josh into a semi-psychotic, B-movie stalker.

Exhibit A.

As a sophomore, Josh switched into Brandon's p.e. class for the sole purpose of watching his dreamboat participate in athletics.

Exhibit B.

That summer Brandon worked as a replacement lifeguard at a local beach club during a holiday weekend. When Josh learned of this, he immediately purchased a week's membership and rented a poolside lounge chair. Sadly, sun poisoning and severe dehydration forced Josh from his dream vacation after only a day and a half (and adding insult to injury, when he sought first aid at the club, Brandon had been on his lunch break).

Exhibit C.

As a junior, Josh again switched into Brandon's p.e. class for the sole purpose of watching his dreamboat participate in athletics.

Exhibit D.

Josh has amassed (à la Samantha) a collection of shirtless photographs of Brandon—at the lake, playing basketball, at the beach club, in his bedroom (I don't even want to think about how he got those)—many of which now line the back of Josh's locker and the top of his bedroom vanity.

Exhibit E.

As a senior, Josh has yet again switched into Brandon's p.e. class for the sole purpose of watching his dreamboat participate in athletics.

"So what does Josh think about all this?" Brandon asked.

"Oh, he's thrilled and overjoyed. He can't wait to see us at GSA."

"Really?"

"Brandon, please tell me having us join GSA wasn't your brainiac suggestion."

"No!" He waved both arms. "It wasn't. Honest. My dad came up with that one on his own. Didn't exactly expect it either."

"That's just great."

"But it's a pretty smart move on his part, don't you think?"

Phil Bildner

There was no way in hell I was going to agree with him, even if he was right.

Our joining the GSA did serve several purposes. For one thing, it gave instant credibility to the GSA. Two "high-profile" students had suddenly joined the ranks. It also diversified a homogenous membership. Up to now, everyone in GSA had either been a straight girl or a gay boy. Lastly, having Brandon and me as members could help to ease the group's militant edge. By this point, I was no longer the only one at Finley who felt Josh needed to chill and bring things down a notch—or twenty.

"Josh is going to be a bigger problem than you think." I glared at him.

"What does that mean?"

"For one thing, he's issued an ultimatum."

"An ultimatum?"

"Yeah. For starters, he said you're not to be at GSA."

"Bullshit," Brandon said defiantly. "It's not up to him."

"That's exactly what I said, but I don't think you really understand Josh and—"

"Let me handle Josh."

"That's not such a good idea." I grimaced and shook my head. "You're not exactly his favorite person at the moment."

"Don't worry about it. I'll handle it. I'll take—"

"No!" I surprised myself at how loudly the word came out. "Listen, Brandon, Josh and I haven't exactly been on speaking terms lately, and this GSA stuff is only making matters worse. Much worse. You don't know him like I do. You don't understand what he's prepared to do."

"Which is what?"

"I don't know."

"Oh, that makes a lot of sense."

I paused and exhaled. "If we join the GSA, he will get us. Trust me, he'll expose me, you, your dad. He'll make sure everyone knows about this. *Everyone*."

"So we screw ourselves if we go, and we screw over my dad if we don't."

"Yes and no."

"You're not making any sense."

"Josh won't do anything today. Not at this meeting. I know how he works. He might make a little scene, make us squirm a little, but he's not ready. He'll want . . . Josh'll want maximum embarrassment and humiliation. We should be safe today. Showing up today only lights the fuse."

"Should? That's reassuring."

"Actually, it is."

"Huh?"

"It buys us time." I looked at my watch. "Speaking of which, we should get going."

"Does that mean I'm no longer being held hostage?"

I reached into the sink, turned on the faucet, and before he had time to react, I splashed him. "Payback!"

Brandon jumped away, but not before I watered him well.

"So are there any other twists I should know about before we go?" Brandon asked. "Anyone else know about our little secret?"

"No."

"Good, I wouldn't let too many people in on the truth."

"So you're telling me to be a closeted straight?"

Brandon laughed. "It's not that bad."

"You're such a shit, Brandon. You know that?"

"You only say that 'cause you think I'm cute." His smile remained. Then he took a step closer.

90   Phil Bildner

"*Puh-lease.*" I made a face like I had just guzzled warm, two-week-old milk. "You need to get over yourself."

He took another step toward me. I could count the droplets of water still running off his face.

"I tell you what, Darcy. I'll make a deal with you." Brandon wiped his chin and cheek and tilted his head. "Since I'm partly responsible for this, I'll—"

"Partly? This is *all* your doing!"

"I'll help you." He spoke gently.

"What are you going to do? Set me up with one of your ex-girlfriends?"

"I'm serious."

He touched my face with the back of his hand.

I started to melt.

"Darcy, I'll make sure this doesn't get out of hand."

His face was so close I could feel the warmth of his lips. I tried to pull away, but I couldn't. I couldn't move. I could barely even speak. "Thanks anyway, Brandon," I managed to say, "but I can take care of myself."

"No, Darcy. I want to."

He ran his fingers down my cheek.

My knees began to buckle.

"We have to get going." I shook my head. "We . . . we can't walk in late."

His lips grazed mine.

And then he pulled away.

"You're right. We can't be late, and I still have to pop back into the lounge for a sec. Wait for me outside the meeting. Give me two minutes."

16

I waited five. Brandon stood me up.

So much for his I'll-help-you-I'll-make-sure-this-doesn't-get-out-of-hand bullshit.

I walked into the meeting, and as expected, every set of eyes turned to me the moment I stepped through the door. I should have felt comfortable and welcome (that is the premise behind GSA, isn't it?), but that was hardly the case.

I smiled politely and made my way to an empty desk in the near corner. There were about a dozen other students present, and considering how small Finely is, I was stunned by the number that were unfamiliar.

Of course, I recognized Gilberto Mills, the club's vice president and Josh's number-one yes-man (or should I say, yes-person in this venue). Josh can't stand Gilberto, but he loves having him as vice president because the boy can't think for himself and only does what others tell him to do. Conveniently, this frees Josh of a significant portion of the menial tasks and drudge work associated with student club administration. Still, like any skilled leader, Josh does throw Gilberto the occasional bone here and there to make him feel worthy.

Gilberto was talking with Mr. Bitner, the GSA's faculty adviser. Body language alone told me that Mr. Bitner couldn't get far enough away from that conversation. Too bad Gilberto didn't get that message until Mr. Bitner, who takes a very hands-off approach in his role with GSA, literally shoved Gilberto toward the front of the room.

Gilberto called the meeting to order—it's one of the bones Josh throws his way. In fact, Josh purposely arrives a couple minutes late to all meetings in order to perpetuate Gilberto's belief that he is a meaningful contributor.

So Josh claims.

If you ask me, Josh purposely arrives a couple minutes late to all meetings so that he can make a grand entrance. Josh *must* be noticed. Yes, give a queen a stage.

Of course, Brandon arrived at the exact moment Gilberto finally had everyone's attention. He walked in with Leslie White, the GSA's treasurer and secretary. She escorted him to a seat by the window like a celebrity being ushered to his luxury box.

Puh-lease.

Leslie is Josh's nemesis. Yes, add her to the ever-growing list of individuals Josh has issues with. Leslie and Josh don't see eye-to-eye on anything remotely related to GSA business, and like most teenagers and hip-hop artists, they're unable to distinguish between political differences and personal hatred (have you noticed the recurring theme yet with Josh?). In fact, right before—and even while—the Darcy-Josh friendship was in its disintegration phase, I was receiving daily you-won't-believe-what-Leslie-wants tantrums and reports of raise-the-roof arguments and near fisticuffs. At present, I'm out of the loop on how far relations have deteriorated and how far this war has escalated, but something told me I was going to find out.

As for Brandon, he didn't even see me as he paraded in. That didn't bother me, but the fact that he didn't even look around the room for me bothered me like nobody's business.

Gilberto greeted the group, thanked everyone for coming, and commented on the large turnout.

"We also have some new members today," he added, "but since we have a lengthy agenda, we're going to hold off until the end to do introductions."

He nodded and waved toward Brandon.

Brandon waved back and then acknowledged the other students. That's when he spotted me. He smiled.

I turned away.

Then Josh walked in. He headed for the front of the room, but stopped dead in his tracks the instant he spotted Brandon. For five seconds—a legitimate five seconds—Josh just stood there.

Then he spotted me.

Suffice it to say, if looks could kill, both Brandon and I would be six feet under.

I couldn't sink far enough down in my seat.

Too bad the same couldn't be said for Brandon. He interpreted Josh's daggers as some kind of testosterone challenge because at that moment he stood up, patted Leslie on the shoulder, and took his sweet time crossing the room before sliding into the seat to my left.

Why are you provoking him?

"Time is money, so let's talk money!" Josh announced, breaking the deafening silence. He dropped some papers on Mr. Bitner's desk and thanked Gilberto for starting the meeting. Then he faced the room and rubbed his hands together like a dice player waiting on his lucky roll.

Wow. I was right . . . so it seemed. Josh wasn't going to do anything. Not now, anyway. He had a meeting to conduct, and that's what he was going to do. Take charge at GSA. Like he always did.

So I hoped. And prayed.

"Our recent fund-raising efforts have been very successful," Josh began. "Last week's bake sale exceeded expectations and raised a hundred and ten dollars. Which is probably more than any Finley sports team ever raised at a bake sale. Way to go."

Josh's news was greeted by applause, soft whistles, and cheers. While his backhanded little dig at Brandon and me was over-looked. More were on the way. I was certain.

"Rest assured," he continued, "from now on, only bake sales. No more car washes!"

Everyone laughed. Even me.

Last year, GSA's fund-raiser car wash turned into a disaster of epic proportions. One car was left in drive and rolled into the side of a Dumpster, another car's windshield was shattered by a squeegee, the water hose broke, and to top it all off, torrential rains poured down all day. The end result: The GSA finished the day seventy-five dollars in the hole.

A folded piece of paper landed on my desk.

"Open it," Brandon whispered.

I ignored him.

"Open it," he said.

I didn't want him to call attention our way, so I did.

SORRY

I so wanted to smile, but I wouldn't let myself. I couldn't. I was still fuming about being stood up *and* ignored. I couldn't let him know his adorable apology had brought back those melting and weak-in-the-knees feelings from the boys' bathroom.

Without even glancing in Brandon's direction, I folded the paper, tucked it into my notebook, and looked back up at Josh.

Good, Darcy. Bonus points for self-control.

"Next, I'm pleased to report the guidance office, at long last, has finally done some updating." Josh picked up pamphlets from the desk. "They finally have materials on hepatitis prevention and inoculations that were created after the Clinton administration. Now we all know none of us can ever contract hep, only our friends can. So tell your friends. And if you want to do some real community service, get at least one friend to read these materials." He paused before adding, "But if your friend is an athlete, you'll probably have to read it *to* him."

Dig number two.

"May I say something?" Leslie White hopped off her windowsill perch.

Uh-oh.

"No, you can't," Josh replied. "You need to wait till the end of the—"

"No, I need to say this now," she interrupted, "especially in light of the sarcastic tone you've opted to take."

Double uh-oh.

"Ms. White, you are out of order. Wait your turn."

"Don't take that condescending approach with me, Josh. I won't stand for your rudeness."

"I'm being rude?" Josh placed a hand on his chest. "I'm not the one commandeering this meeting and violating every rule of order."

You know how Samantha turns Josh into a fourth grader? Well, Leslie does the same thing, but with Leslie it generally happens in the presence of others—many others.

Leslie faced the group. "It's important that we welcome our new members. It's *rude* to wait till the end."

Ooh!

Phil Bildner

"Ms. White, the floor doesn't belong to you." Josh was raising his voice. "You need to sit down. If you have an issue regarding the introduction of newcomers, bring it up as a point—"

"I don't have an issue." Leslie refused to back off. "It's called being polite. Common courtesy. Something you obviously don't have a clue about."

Look out!

Suddenly Josh's hands and arms were flailing. "And who are we being polite to?" His head twitched twice. "Are you so naïve as to actually think these *newcomers*, who you've hoisted onto a pedestal, are actually here on their own volition?"

For the first time since he sat down next to me, I allowed myself to peek at Brandon. He was as intrigued and entertained by the bickering and tension as I was.

Then he looked back at me. And then . . .

Eye lock.

That awkward moment of eye contact when you're trying to catch someone's eye, but you really don't want them to know that you're trying to catch their eye.

Oh, my god.

Eye lock.

It lasted only a second, perhaps even less, but I knew Brandon experienced it too.

I felt weak. I was done. Toast.

I turned back to the battle royal, but I was no longer able to process anything going on between Leslie and Josh (and god, I wish I had been, because I later learned that things escalated to the point where Mr. Bitner actually had to step between the two combatants). I don't even know how long I sat there. It could have been twenty seconds or twenty minutes.

It didn't matter.

When I returned from my state of suspended animation, the meeting was in the process of dispersing, and I was staring up at Josh, hovering over me like an old lady over a child who had just trampled through her flower bed. Both his hands were on the desk where I sat, and he was leaning so far in that I could smell the banana nut muffin he had eaten before the meeting.

"You thought I was playing, BSB, didn't you?"

I had just returned to earth, so I wasn't prepared with a comeback.

"What's it going to take, BSB?" he snarled through gritted teeth. "How many times do we have to go through this in order for you to take me seriously?"

I swallowed.

"Now watch, BSB. Just watch. It's time for you to get a taste of real life. I swear to god, you will *never* play a single baseball game!"

Am I going through with this or not?

I refuse to leave this car until I decide once and for all. I don't care if I have to sit in here all day. I'm not going back to class until I've made up my mind.

Do I really want to pretend to be a lesbian my senior year? My senior year! The best year of my life!

Brandon Basset, you suck! You suck for doing this to me, and you suck for being so damn hot. I hate that I like you. But you know what, Brandon? I'm playing baseball and reducing you to platoon status. You deserve everything headed your way. You don't deserve to be spared shit!

You suck too, Josh! You bitter little queen, you're gonna keep your mouth shut if I have to see to it personally. You're gonna ruin this for me? I don't think so. Try it. I dare you. No way are you ruining this for me. This is my dream. You're not messing with it.

Nathalie.

I have to tell Nathalie. I can't spend the next months lying to her. The woman gets suspicious the moment I close my bedroom door. She's gonna wig! Of course, she's gonna wig. Is there anything she doesn't wig about? God, knowing her, she'll be the one to out me. My own freakin' mother!

This is freakin' surreal. Shit like this doesn't happen. Not in the real world. Well, this isn't the real world. This is high school.

What if I can't handle it? What if it's too much? What if it's all too overwhelming? Then what?

C'mon, Darcy, you can do this. You want this. Yes, you can do this. You know you can. This can be fun. This will be fun. And this is a good thing. You're going to be doing good. A lot of good. Opening eyes. Think of the "wonderful effects this will have on the entire community."

Okay, holy freakin' martyr complex.

Yes, I have to do this. This is what I want. To play baseball. That's all I ever wanted. All these other things are just going to be things I'll have to deal with. And I will deal with them. Minor inconveniences. Bumps in the road. Little things that are going to keep things interesting.

Keep telling yourself that, Darcy.

I just want to play for the baseball team. Take the field. Hear my name announced.

That would be plenty. It's that simple.

"Now batting: Darcy Miller."

18

Despite my near breakdown, I managed to make it to practice that afternoon. While I was still a little nervous, I was more excited and fired up than anything else.

Like the previous day, the practice started with a team stretch, but as soon as we finished this time, Irv sent me right to batting practice on the main diamond since he hadn't seen me take any cuts yet. Theoretically, I was still trying out for the team. So far I had only demonstrated that I could pitch. What if I wasn't able to do anything else?

Right.

I was still in recovery mode from my latest episode of cerebral suffocation, so this was exactly what I needed.

I grabbed my helmet and gloves, picked up the lightest bat I could find, and stepped to the plate. I heard a few whispers and felt more than a few eyes, and while the day before that had bothered and concerned me (especially with what happened with ICBM), today I welcomed it. This was going to be *my* team. Bro had made that perfectly clear, and if anyone still wasn't aware of that, they were about to find out now.

I took Irv's first pitch. That's something you *never* do during bp. During batting practice, you swing at everything close, especially when there's a snaking line of hitters waiting. The pitch had been perfect, and letting it go drew heckles from the three junior-varsity players standing in front of the protective fence by the visitors' bench:

"Darcy's mom gives good brain!"

Followed by:

"Maybe if my mom blows the principal, I can blow off my chem labs!"

And followed by:

"Hey, boys, *les-bee* nice to Butchie. She might kick our ass."

Showtime!

I relaxed my hands and grip. That's my key to hitting, or should I say that's *the* key to hitting?

Irv delivered again.

Whack!

A scorching line drive to left.

I glanced over at Larry, Moe, and Curly. Silenced. I smiled and nodded.

Showtime! Take two!

I took a half step away from the plate and dug back in. I needed to be able to extend my arms for this next pitch.

"What do roaches do when you turn on the lights?" I asked the catcher without turning around.

"What do what?" he replied.

Irv rocked into his delivery.

"This!"

I swung and laced a foul ball right at my three amigos. They scampered and scattered like roaches when the lights go on.

I turned back to the catcher, smiled, and nodded. He was obviously impressed.

God, I love the fact that I can direct foul balls. I don't know of many players who can, and I definitely don't know of any who can do it as well as I can. Comes in quite handy sometimes.

"Straighten it out, Lassie!" Bro called from the dugout.

So I did.

I drilled the next pitch right at Irv's feet, up the middle for what would have been a clean base hit. And for the remainder of my swings, I made solid contact on every pitch, spraying the ball all over the field.

Go me!

When I finished my cuts, I took off my helmet, shook out my hair, walked right over to my silenced hecklers sitting *behind* the fence, and sat down on the bench between them. Didn't say a word. Didn't have to.

This was going to be fun!

Unfortunately, I didn't get to bask in the glow for long because both Irv and Bro wanted to see what else I could do, and for the remainder of practice those two followed me like state troopers following an Escalade on the New Jersey Turnpike.

And I knew why. This was PR work at its finest. I was being showcased, paraded around so everyone could see I wasn't here simply because my mom and the principal were getting it on. Irv and Bro needed everyone to see their new diamond in the rough.

First, they wanted to see me take pfp, pitcher's fielding practice.

"Bro, I think I may need some work pitching from the stretch," I told him on the way out to the utility mounds and makeshift infield on the football field. While I was more than happy to oblige their show-and-tell charade, I couldn't completely let on that I knew exactly what was going on.

But Bro simply laughed at my lame attempt. "Lassie, you let me worry 'bout that. Right now, we wanna watch you gobble grounders."

"But my delivery's too slow with runners on base, and they're going to be able to run on me at—"

"Lassie, I'm tellin' ya, you let me worry 'bout that," Bro repeated. "Reckon, with your stuff, y'ain't ever gonna be workin' from the stretch." Bro glanced at Irv and chuckled. "You throw like you done yesterday, and I'll be countin' on these here digits how many times runners git on base 'gainst you all season!" He pointed to my glove. "Right now, Lassie, grounders."

I appreciated his confidence, I really did, but even I (yes, even I) felt Bro was overstating things.

Still, if all they wanted to see was me fielding comebackers to the mound . . .

Grounders to my right. No prob.

Grounders to my left. Cake.

Random comebackers. All fielded cleanly.

Once again, the siblings were more than extremely pleased.

Next they wanted to see how I did covering first base on ground-balls to the right side of the infield. This is the play *every* pitcher needs to master. It's common baseball sense that on balls hit to the right side of the infield, a pitcher must instantly break for first. Still it's amazing how many pitchers fail to react automatically, and all it takes is one hesitation or hiccup and any runner of moderate speed will beat the pitcher to the bag.

I was butter . . . again.

Bro and Irv then had me try some double plays: first, the 1-6-3 double play, where the pitcher fields and whirls to second to start the play, and then the less common 3-6-1 double play, where the groundball is fielded by the first baseman, who throws to second for the first out, and the relay throw back to first is caught by the covering pitcher.

Another clinic courtesy of Darcy Miller.

"Bro, what about holding runners on?" I pressed again. I felt that a sufficient amount of time (maybe eighteen to twenty minutes) had passed since I had last raised my concern.

"Lassie, what'd I say to you b'fore?"

"But if I'm always pitching from a full windup, everyone who gets on is going to run on me."

Bro scratched his head exasperatedly. "Tell you what. If it'll make you happy, the day before the opener 'gainst Danforth, come to me. I'll show you a slide step."

"A slide step? What's that?"

"How 'bout that!" He turned to Irv. "Finally somethin' the girl don' know. Mind if I show her real quick?"

"Go right ahead," Irv replied.

"Lassie, the slide step is real simple. Real simple." Bro stepped to the mound. "It's a basic move to the plate. You come to yer set like you usually do, but instead of rockin' into your delivery, you slide forward." He demonstrated in slow motion. "You throw yer pitch without the leg kick."

I imitated the mechanics. "Won't that take away some of my velocity?"

"Lassie, you don't throw so hard to begin with, so you don't gotta worry 'bout that. And I reckon since you don't throw 'er no hook neither, we don't gotta worry 'bout you hangin' no fat Uncle Charlies." He flipped me the ball. "You satisfied now?"

Before I had the chance to try the move or even reply, Irv had draped his arm around me.

"Darcy," he said, "why don't you come over to the field with me? That okay with you, Bro?"

Bro clapped and pointed with both hands. "Show 'em who's boss, Lassie!"

I saluted Bro with my glove.

"Darcy, how you holding up?" Irv kept his arm around me as we walked.

"So far, so good," I replied, although I felt awkward and uncomfortable with his heavy arm weighing me down. I couldn't squirm away if I wanted to.

"Anybody giving you a hard time?"

"Just that one incident yesterday."

"Yeah, Bro told me about that. Said you handled yourself pretty good."

"Thanks."

"Nobody else?"

"There's been an occasional comment, and I've definitely gotten my share of looks and glares, but that's to be expected."

God, I was so working it. Even without a dad, I was quite adept at giving the paternal guy exactly what he wanted. The father figure wanted to feel like he was there for his little girl. I was happy to oblige (again). Where was the harm?

"Think you're ready to handle a little more?" he asked.

"How so?"

Irv stopped walking so he could face me. "You ready to give short a shot?"

This was too good to be true. Brandon was about to get some. Maybe not the *some* he originally envisioned getting from me, but, oh yes, he was about to get a taste of Darcy Miller.

"Does Brandon know?" I asked.

Irv shook his head.

My smile widened. I couldn't have scripted this better if I had penned it myself.

"You haven't said anything?"

Irv was smiling now too. He held out his hand.

"You can have the honors, Darcy."

19

Before even giving myself a hint of a chance to lose my nerve, I trotted toward short, where Brandon was soft-tossing with Sam.

"What are you doing out here?" he asked immediately.

"Irv sent me."

"Why?" There was concern in his voice.

"You'll have to ask Irv."

"I'm asking you."

"I play short when I don't pitch." I faced home plate and wind-milled my throwing arm, preparing for my first set of grounders.

"*What?*" Brandon stepped around me, blocking my view of Irv, who was readying himself in the batter's box.

"You heard me."

"No, I don't think I did."

I peered around Brandon as Irv sent the first groundball to the right side of the infield.

Brandon glanced back toward Irv, and I took a few steps toward second, purposely playing a little game of cat-and-mouse peekaboo.

"Why short?" Brandon followed me. "Why not the outfield or something?"

"Short's my best position. You know that."

Irv motioned with his bat that the next ball was coming my way.

With an exaggerated, backhanded motion of my glove, I instructed Brandon to slide over. It was fun teasing him in a way that jocks never get teased.

"But I'm the starting shortstop." More concern in his tone.

"Uh-huh."

"You know that."

"Uh-huh."

"Irv knows about this?"

"Uh-huh."

"And Bro?"

"Uh-huh."

I slide-stepped in front of Brandon, fielded my grounder cleanly, and fired a pea to first.

"No way," Brandon steamed. "Not on this team."

"Uh-huh." I held out my hand and graciously allowed him to take the next ball.

"I've started at short the last two years. You can't just come in like that."

"Don't whine, Brandon. People might get the wrong idea about you, even though you say that could never happen."

"I'm the starting shortstop," he repeated.

"Gee, that's a little selfish of you, don't you think? Putting your interests before the team's? But if that is how you want to look at things, consider this my tryout. Let's see what happens."

Brandon was at a complete loss for words. Fortunately for him, Irv sent a grounder his way. He backhanded the ball and sidearmed his throw to first.

"Put something on that throw!" Irv shouted.

I covered my face with my glove. Here I was in the process of shattering the Ego King, and Irv was criticizing his effort. That's gotta sting.

"You knew about this all along, didn't you, Darcy?"

"Uh-huh."

"Stop with the friggin' uh-huhs already."

I still had my glove over my face hiding my I-sure-did smile.

"You set me up, Darcy. When did you know about this?"

"The same day your daddy said I could play. I told Irv that afternoon."

"Irv's known all along?"

"It would appear that way, Brandon, now wouldn't it?"

"Don't be a bitch!"

"Easy! No need for name-calling." I lowered my glove from my face and stepped around him to field my next groundball as routinely as the first.

"How could you spring something like this on me?"

"How could *I* spring something like this on *you*? You've got to be kidding? Look what you did to me!"

"Is that what this is about?" Brandon raised his voice. "You're trying to get me back? You're trying to punish me?"

"This isn't about punishing you. It just happens to be one of the perks."

"You are being such a bitch! You know that?"

I did. But I had a really good reason to be a bitch. A *really* good one. Actually several, but one in particular that justified my behavior and attitude: It was my primary defense mechanism.

While I was oozing confidence on the outside, I wasn't nearly as self-assured on the inside. I mean, don't get me wrong. I was plenty confident in my capabilities, but I was nervous. I admit it. My "being such a bitch" was my way of acting out, as my mom,

Sam, and every other person who has gotten to know me at all from the age of thirteen to the present likes to call it.

"Tell you what." I was still dripping sarcasm. "I'll help you through this. Kinda like the way you said you'd help me. You know, this could be fun."

"You're ruining . . . my . . . my life."

"*Puh-lease*, Brandon." I bust out laughing. "Your life? Ease up on the melodramatics. You're losing your starting spot on the baseball team. Big deal." I paused, and then said deliberately, "It's not like someone's outing you to the entire student body."

Brandon tucked his glove under his arm and pointed in my face. "Let me tell you something, Darcy. This crossed a line."

"And what line is that, Brandon?"

"I'm not helping you out with this lesbian thing anymore."

"Like you've helped me so much to this point." I swatted his finger away.

"And I have news for you, Darcy. I don't regret what I did either."

"Oh, Brandon, don't get all bitter, pissy, and vindictive. It's so not attractive." I stepped closer. "Now I have some news for *you*. If you know what's good for you, you'll be careful about Josh and the GSA. Josh isn't going to be satisfied with just coming after me. He's coming after you and your dad."

"Well then, you'd better do something about that psycho friend of yours." Brandon stepped in so our faces were as close as they had been in the boys' bathroom (though the feelings we were experiencing now were decidedly dissimilar). "You've got another thing coming if you think you're taking shortstop from me."

"What are you going to do, Brandon? Tell your daddy?"

Now in my seventeen years of living, I have *never* gotten beaten up. Sure I've gotten into a few scraps here and there (who hasn't?), but at no time did anyone ever kick the shit out of me. Well, I was certain that was all about to change. Brandon's fists were clenched, and his eyes were so buggin' I didn't know if his eye sockets could hold them. Yes, if ever there was a moment when I would have understood another person losing it on me, it was then.

But no.

Brandon simply backed away.

And for the remainder of practice, Brandon didn't say a word, for he understood the reality of the situation. His very status on the team *and* his reputation were at stake.

Because of a girl. And not just any girl. Me. Darcy Miller.

Brandon Basset didn't have a prayer.

Ouch.

I fielded every groundball hit my way. One play, a sliding stop on a ball hit to my right followed by a long throw from my knees, drew a "Terrific play!" from Irv and applause from Sam over at second.

Brandon made several nice plays too, including a diving stop of a ball hit behind second. But he also let a few balls play him. One ball skipped over his shoulder, and two others scooted through his legs.

After the second miscue, he kicked the dirt, accidentally sending pebbles into Sam.

God, I was so inside his head.

I smirked behind my glove and remembered back to my so-right thoughts when Principal Braindead had first informed me I was a lesbian: Situations don't dictate Darcy Miller. Darcy Miller dictates situations.

20

During cool downs at the end of practice, Irv called Brandon and me over behind the backstop.

"I'm not gonna mince words here. I'm just gonna come out and say this." Irv rested his arms on his belly and faced Brandon. "Brandon, I like what I see in the new kid. She doesn't make errors. Her throws are crisp and accurate, and she turns the double play better than anyone I've seen at the high school level."

"Irv, it's only been two days," Brandon said calmly, "and these are practices. You don't know how she's going to do in a game. How can you decide—"

"Now, son," Irv placed a steadying hand on Brandon's shoulder, "nothing's etched in stone here, but it's a short preseason. We're less than ten days from our opener."

"You're jumping the gun."

"Maybe so, but when Darcy's not pitching, I'm puttin' her at short and moving you to the outfield."

I so wanted to gloat. I swear to god, I wanted to perform an end-zone touchdown celebration, but I was able to ward off that overwhelming impulse . . . for now.

"You can't do that. I've never played the outfield." A faint whine crept into Brandon's voice.

"I know you're disappointed—"

"Irv, I'm a senior!"

"I don't care if you're Ichiro or A-Rod! I'm disappointed in the attitude, Brandon."

Ouch. That had to sting.

Brandon glared daggers at me.

"Then we're set." Irv picked his clipboard off the bench and tucked it under his arm. "I'll see you two tomorrow."

I waited until Irv was out of earshot before turning to Brandon.

"I guess this makes you versatile."

"Kiss my ass, Darcy."

"Not interested anymore. I'm a lesbian now, remember?" This was a hoot.

"Go to hell, Darcy. This isn't over."

"Exactly, Brandon, that's what I've been trying to tell you. So before you go losing your shit any more than you already have, you need to watch out for Josh. Take him seriously."

"That 'mo can also go to hell." Brandon headed off.

I waited until he was safely beyond striking-back range before delivering my parting shot.

"Hey, Brandon! No hard feelings. I'm still more than willing to teach you everything you need to know to back me up."

I headed home. I had one more thing to take care of.

Nathalie.

She had to know. I couldn't risk her finding out about all this on the supermarket checkout line or while picking up the dry cleaning. I had to tell her now.

But when I got home, I was greeted by another we-have-to-talk Post-it, this one affixed to the box of brown sugar Pop-Tarts (my fave) strategically wedged into the refrigerator door handle. I immediately called out for Sequel (aka Legsy II, although nothing will ever compare to my first dog), and when I heard the jingle of her dog tags, I felt relieved knowing this "we have to talk" wouldn't be about another dead pet.

Still I was concerned. Was it possible that in the hour since practice Brandon had managed to get to Nathalie? Or had someone else told her that the reason I could play for the baseball team was because, oh by the way, I was a lesbian?

I pondered the note and concluded that Nathalie had written it before she went to work. Nevertheless, the mere thought of Brandon retaliating through Nathalie reinforced my belief that I needed to beef up homeland security.

When Nathalie walked in an hour later, I was in the living room playing my PS2, and one look at her told me she had had one of those days.

"Don't even ask," she said, blowing me a kiss, tossing her bag on the floor, and plopping down on the couch.

So I didn't.

One thing I've learned is *never* try talking to Nathalie the moment she walks in from work. No good can come of it. Let her initiate conversation. God knows, she'll talk when she's ready.

So I went back to my video game.

"You get my note?"

Despite her apparently awful day, Nathalie was still ready to converse less than eight seconds later.

I nodded.

"Can you shut that thing off so I can talk to you about something?"

I complied.

That's another thing I've learned. Whenever Nathalie gets home from work and makes a request that's not completely unreasonable, it's in my best interest to honor it.

"What's up?" I sat down on the couch beside her.

Nathalie rubbed her temples. "It's about Bill and me."

"Is everything okay?" I tried to sound like I cared.

"Oh, yeah. It's nothing like that. It's just . . ."

He didn't tell her. He promised he wouldn't.

I picked up a sofa cushion and braced myself for the worst.

"Bill asked me to go away with him for a weekend."

"And?"

"And that's it."

"That's it?"

"That's it."

I was genuinely surprised. Well, shocked was more like it. Considering I was expecting a so-you're-gay-and-you-can't-even-tell-your-own-mother cataclysmic bombshell.

"What's the big deal?" I asked.

"Well, I didn't know how you'd take it."

How did you think I would take it? I'm seventeen, and you're leaving me home alone for the weekend.

"I'm glad you're okay with it. That's definitely a load off my mind."

Now was my chance. This was my opportunity. So as I learned in Latin class and from *The Simpsons* . . .

Carpe diem.

"Mom, there's something I need to talk to you about."

"Anything." She reached over and stroked my hair.

I exhaled. "I have a problem."

Boom!

"Are you pregnant? Darcy, if you're pregnant, I think—"

"Pregnant? Mom! I'm not pregnant." I placed my hand firmly on her leg. "I'm not pregnant. Calm down!"

I'm the only one on the planet allowed to say "calm down" to her, and even I assume the risk when I do.

"Do I need to fix myself a drink?" She placed her hand over her chest.

My mother, the role model.

"No," I answered uncertainly, "you can handle this."

Nathalie still clutched her chest as she breathed a set of Dr. St. Claire *longdeeplongdeeplongdeep* breaths. "Talk to me. What's the matter?"

"It's hard to explain. But it has to do with baseball."

"Are you having second thoughts? After what we went through, are you—"

"Mom! Shut up!" I shouted so loud Sequel yelped and scampered from the room. "Yes, I still want to play baseball. Now will you chill?" I stood up. "Maybe you should get that drink."

"No, Darcy. I'm fine. Really I am. Go on now. Tell me."

I stood over her. "Mom, do you know why Principal Basset's letting me play baseball?"

"Of course I do."

"You do?"

"Yes, Bill and I spoke about it at length."

"Okay." I looked at her oddly. "What exactly did he tell you?"

"The same thing he told you. He said he gave a lot of thought to what I told him the other day in his office—"

"No, Mom, it's not."

". . . and he realized not allowing you to play baseball made no sense."

"It's not."

"You would only help the team, so he decided to let—"

"No, Mom! It's not!"

"What do you mean, *It's not?*"

"I mean there's more to it than that."

"So you're telling me Bill lied to me?"

I shook my head. "I wouldn't go that far."

"Then what exactly are you telling me, Darcy?"

I exhaled. "The real reason he's letting me play is because of something Brandon told him."

"I think you're mistaken, Darcy. Bill made it very clear to me just last night that what I had said to him—"

"Mom!" I leaned over and placed both my hands on her shoulders to brace her. "Brandon told Principal Basset I'm gay. Your boyfriend, my principal, thinks I'm a lesbian."

Never in my life had I seen Nathalie with such an expression of distress and disbelief, and it was only after three glasses of water, six mouthed oh-my-gods, and numerous consecutive repetitions of Dr. St. Claire breathing that she finally reacquired the ability to speak.

"You're gay, Darcy?"

"No, Mom. I'm not." I had my arm around her and spoke like I was trying to calm a panicked parent (which I was).

"Are you sure you're not gay?"

"Positive. But that's what Brandon told his father."

"What would possess Brandon to say such a thing?"

I smiled. "Let's just say Brandon has a very active imagination."

Slowly and steadily, I recounted the events of the last two days. Several times along the way, Nathalie tried to interrupt, but I wouldn't let her. I needed to get this out. I needed her to hear my side. The truth.

When I finally reached the end of my saga, I took a Dr. St. Claire *longdeeplongdeeplongdeep* breath. It was time to drop the next part of my big bomb.

"Mom, there's one more thing."

"I'm listening."

Another *longdeeplongdeeplongdeep* breath.

"You might not like this."

"I'm still listening."

"I need you to play along."

"Excuse me?"

I nodded. "I need you to play along."

"Play along?"

"Principal Basset can't know I'm straight."

"Oh, I don't know, Darcy. I can't be dishonest to Bill. I can't lie to him. A relationship based on dishonesty is doomed for—"

"I'm not asking you to lie." I cut her off even though that's *exactly* what I was asking her to do. "All I'm saying is don't volunteer anything."

"I don't know, Darcy."

"Please, Mom. You know how much I love baseball."

"Yes, I've lived with you for seventeen years. I should know better than anyone."

"Then you know how much this means to me. Please." I said with the perfect amount of whining and begging.

"And what do I get in return?" Nathalie made a face one would expect to see from me (I guess I inherited that trait, too).

I paused. "You get my blessing to go away for the weekend with Bill."

"You already gave me your blessing."

I had, hadn't I?

I put my arm around her and kissed her cheek. "Okay, you get to share in a little mother-daughter fun."

"I don't know, Darcy," she repeated.

I could tell Nathalie was wavering, and all it took were four more "Please, Mom" whines and a Stoli on the rocks before she acquiesced.

Natalie Miller is the coolest mom in the world. She has her hang-ups, but let's face it: How many moms do you know would date the principal, threaten the principal to let her daughter play boys' baseball, and then not reveal to the principal her daughter's closeted heterosexuality?

I ask you, how many?

22

Finley is a relatively small high school, so word of the "Darcy Miller situation" spread faster than head lice through a kindergarten class.

As far as practices went, I was in a playpen. Nothing bad could possibly happen to me there. I was in a perfectly safe environment, insulated from all harm. In essence, it was sanitized gay living. Not only did everyone know of my sexuality, but I also had everyone's stamp of approval. No one dared to disapprove, for if they did, they risked being more ostracized than a gay person in the real world.

However . . . just because attacks on my supposed sexual orientation were off-limits didn't mean *everything* was off-limits. The digs at my other skeleton in the closet (note the so-intended pun) still ran rampant.

"Who's your daddy, Darcy?"

Followed by:

"Give us the dirt, Darcy: Is Bill a grunter, a moaner, or a groaner?"

And followed by:

"Got any home movies, Darcy?"

Big deal. Everyone gives everyone shit about something at every practice. That's part of high school athletics everywhere.

The only real over-and-above thing I had to contend with at

practice were some extra glances and stares, and in the grand scheme of things, big deal again.

So what if the middle schoolers waited for the buses by the baseball diamonds instead of in the parking lot? So what if the students staying after school for clubs and activities gawked out the classroom windows? And so what if every other varsity athlete on the way to practice stopped to sneak a peek at the lesbo playing with the boys?

But if practice was a protected playpen, then Finley was a wide-open playground where every day—every moment—was field day on Darcy Miller.

Yes, it was anything goes.

Okay, now's where you'll have to indulge me. We've reached the self-reflection and introspection portion of these proceedings. . . .

Let me tell you, the abuse one must endure when the student body of your high school learns that your mom is the object of your principal's affection is pretty brutal, but it's nothing compared to having your "deviant" sexual preference become public knowledge. Nothing. When the student body learns you're a card-carrying member of the lesbian race, all bets are off.

Now in light of everything that's happened between Josh and me, one would think I wouldn't want to admit to this. And I don't. But I will.

Cognizance.

I hate that freakin' word. Because I hate how right Josh is.

You're constantly conscious of who you are and of what you are, and there's no escape. No matter what the situation and scenario, in high school you are always aware of your sexuality. And so is everyone else.

That's what I never bought into. That's what Josh always tried to tell me, but I categorically dismissed it.

Sexuality was never a problem for me. It didn't matter. It *doesn't* matter, or at least it *shouldn't* matter. That's the way I always approached it. Any other approach is illogical.

But now I see that just because I'm okay with it, and I think about it logically, doesn't mean everyone else does. Because everyone else doesn't. And because everyone else isn't okay with it, you feel like you're doing something wrong.

Got all that?

I keep asking myself this other question: What if I wasn't a good player? What if I was just some marginal player who wanted to play boys' baseball? Would I still be allowed to play?

No chance.

What a double standard. Double standards. Double standards become so obvious and apparent when they suddenly apply to you, or when you decide to truly open your eyes and acknowledge that which is staring you in the face.

At times, I find I'm comparing myself to star athletes who take steroids or do drugs or beat their spouses. Now let's be *overly* clear: Being gay cannot be grouped into any such category (despite what a sizeable number of members of the House of Representatives would like the public to believe). Nevertheless, similar standards and rules are applied. Those who make decisions and set policy, as well as society as a whole, tend to forgive superstars for their transgressions. So long as they perform on the field and help the team succeed, we forgive—or at least we're willing to look the other way.

An average player would never be treated that way. An average player would never get the opportunity to take the field in the first place, and even if by chance he or she was allowed on the field, reality and society would be far less forgiving of the average player.

Would Principal Basset have reached the same conclusion

about me if I wasn't this good? Was this really part of his thinking?

What is that?

That's that other question I keep coming back to: What is that? What is that all about?

I'll tell you what it is: Reality. It's what Josh has been saying all along.

Nothing has changed about me. I am the same person I was a few days ago except for this new label. Why does that suddenly make me different?

I'll even go one step further (I'm almost done, I promise.): Every kid gets teased and taunted in high school. It's part of the process, part of the rite of passage. But when the gay kid is the target, there's a meanness to it. There's a hate.

I used to recite to Josh the nursery school rhyme, "Sticks and stones may break my bones, but names will never hurt me," and that would always set him off.

"Bullshit, Darcy! Names hurt. Words hurt. They hurt more than you can imagine."

I don't have to imagine now. I know.

Josh, I know.

That's what I want to tell him, but unfortunately in typical Josh fashion he isn't about to make things easy for me.

No, no, no.

Josh wants to prove his point *his* way. It's irrelevant that I might be conceding defeat. He wants to teach me this lesson on his terms, and in the process it doesn't matter if I or anyone else gets hurt because when Josh gets into one of his need-to-turn-things-up-a-notch mindsets, he resembles a crazed stalker (which is what Brandon said, isn't it?).

Josh is going about things this way—intentionally irrational, intolerant, uncontrollable, unforgiving, harsh, and unpredictable—for a reason. Why? Because that's exactly how society is when it targets gays and lesbians.

Tell me I don't know my (former) best friend?

He started with a barrage of flyers the day after the GSA meeting. Each time I returned to my locker, I would find another flyer slipped in, saying, JUDGMENT DAY IS COMING, THE END IS NEAR, or THE TIME IS APPROACHING. All the flyers had different wording, different fonts, and were of varying size and color, but there was no doubt this was Josh's handiwork. They were obviously coming from someone who knew my schedule, because they were there every time I returned to my locker. Plus only Josh could have picked those colors: electric blue, seaweed, hot pink, raspberry, and deep purple.

After two days of these warnings, I was greeted by a large envelope labeled Phase Two slipped underneath my windshield wiper blade.

I sat down in the car and shut the door before opening it.

In a carefully constructed packet, Josh presented evidence of me "cavorting with known heterosexuals." He was proffering concrete proof that my "homosexual orientation was of a questionable nature." After flipping through the pages of anecdotes, hearsay accounts, and personal experiences, I was both impressed by the amount of information he had compiled and unnerved by the amount of time he had on his hands to actually do this.

Unfortunately there was one particularly disturbing item contained in that envelope.

The DVD.

I knew exactly what was on it. It was the footage from that night of silliness last summer, that night when Josh and I played with

Nathalie's new digital video camera and decided to act out our fantasies with the boys on my walls.

Boys on my wall? Yep, the cutouts of *all our* favorite cuties.

Hilarious does not even begin to describe it. So hilarious that we didn't, we *couldn't*, erase it. So hilarious that we made multiple copies.

But we swore no one else was ever going to see it. That was then.

Presently Josh had other plans for those twelve minutes of video, and if it ever came down to it, I was going to have a pretty tough time explaining it.

Of course, Josh refused to answer my calls, at home or on the cell, or even acknowledge my barrage of e-mails, IMs, and text messages.

He did, however, finally pay me a visit at my locker two mornings later.

"Know what these are, BSB?" He held a stack of sealed express-mail envelopes.

"Get out of my face, Josh." I spun my combination. "You're out-bitching Samantha on a heavy-flow day."

"Know what these are?"

"Does it matter?" I was in no mood.

"These are the first shots. The *real* first shots."

"I'm proud of you." I nearly opened the locker into his face. "You having a good time with all this?"

He smiled devilishly. "The buildup is rather amusing."

"Don't you think you've made your point?"

"It's a little different than how you thought it would be, isn't it?"

"I've been trying to tell you that, but you don't want to hear it. How many times do I have to say it?"

"It doesn't matter how many times you say it, BSB. That's the

Phil Bildner

point. What you say and what you do are irrelevant. You don't get to control it."

"So then why are you even talking to me? Why are you wasting your time standing here right now?"

Josh so wanted me to ask about the envelopes, and he was getting irritated that I hadn't.

"That's also part of the fun."

"Whatever, Josh. I'm late for—"

"And when these get sent"—he waved the envelopes—"then you'll—"

"Do you really think people are going to care?" I pulled my math text out from underneath the mound of Josh-handouts. "I'm late for class."

"There's one addressed to each member of the school board." Josh fanned the envelopes. "There's one to every—"

"Who gives a shit, Josh?" I raised my voice.

"There's one to Principal Basset, Brandon, and lookie here, there's even one addressed to BSB herself."

"I'll be checking the mail hourly." I slammed my locker. "What's in them, Josh? That is what you want me to ask, isn't it?"

"Maybe."

"So what's in them? Your X-rated JPEGs from your online friends? Fashion tips for fags? I don't have time for this."

"Exactly, BSB. You don't have time for this, and you can't be bothered, but when you're gay, that choice isn't up to you. That choice is made *for* you."

"And thank you for repeatedly bringing home the message I've already received."

I stormed off.

23

With Josh stressing me out and freaking me out, every hallway glance, every bathroom murmur, and every . . . everything was magnified by the power of many to the point where my paranoia was beginning to cross into the unhealthy range.

Still I was getting to live my baseball fantasy. That's what was keeping me going. Baseball was everything I thought it would be and then some.

I love baseball (I may have let that slip a few times by now). I consider myself a student of the game (okay, I'm a dork), but I don't know nearly as much about the game as Irv does. Irv's type of baseball knowledge develops only over time, so a large part of the baseball nirvana I was experiencing stemmed from watching this master coach teach the game.

Take, for instance, his hit-and-run drill. It addresses nearly every facet of the game simultaneously. For hitters, it provides practice in hitting behind runners and hitting down on the ball. For pitchers, it's the chance to work on holding runners on, throwing to first, working the inside part of the plate to left-handed batters, and pitching away to right-handed batters. For base runners, it's the opportunity to focus on reading pitchers, getting jumps off first, and sliding. And for the fielders, the drill reinforces the basics like cutoff throws and backing up bases.

Genius.

Irv also emphasizes slide work.

"If you think you have to slide, you have to slide," he frequently reminded us. "And better to slide early than late."

Irv also forbids headfirst slides. In his mind, a headfirst slide is tantamount to charging the mound on a hit-by-pitch.

"I've wasted too many nights in emergency rooms for broken fingers, hands, and wrists. You slide headfirst, you sit. End of story."

Then there are Irv's rundown drills, which he always makes us work on at the end of practice.

"Nobody on my field watches a rundown play! Everyone's a participant! Everyone's talking! Force the runner to commit full speed in one direction!"

In theory, the drills should take only a few minutes max. All Irv ever wants is for us to execute five perfect rundowns in a row.

Ha!

One day we were out there an extra twenty-five minutes, and the following day, a Friday afternoon, we were out there an extra thirty! I swear, by the end of those practices, some of the guys definitely wanted to inflict egregious bodily harm on some of the others.

As for me, the baseball geek, I couldn't get enough of this stuff. I would get as juiced as a sugared-up seven-year-old at a sleepover!

Irv also put special emphasis on overlooked aspects of the game. For example, because high school hitters often get fooled, and "excuse me" grounders occur several times a game, he dedicated ten minutes of fielding practice to slow groundballs.

"Three slow groundballs—that's an inning of outs," Irv would say. "Good teams get those outs."

Mesmerized by the intricacies of the game, I (of course) took it upon myself to master the techniques involved.

The key to fielding the slow roller is to field the ball off the inside of the left foot so you can plant the right for the throw. You charge the ball with both hands in front, so if you catch the ball with the glove (instead of barehanding it), your throwing hand is right there for the transfer and submarine throw.

Each time I successfully completed one I was more pumped than the last.

Now with all these multilevel, multiskill, multiplayer drills, it was inevitable that Brandon and I were going to cross paths.

To put it mildly, Brandon was not enjoying himself at practice, and watching me have the time of my life certainly contributed mightily to the depths of his displeasure.

Whenever we were near each other during a drill, Brandon moved away. If we were positioned next to one another, he would always have his back to me or be watching the other players. And when Irv or Bro huddled the team together, Brandon always stood on the outer rim. Sometimes he even stood outside the group, and one time when Irv addressed us behind the pitcher's mound, Brandon actually stood, arms folded, on the edge of the outfield grass!

The tension that existed between Brandon and me was in plain sight. Everyone knew what was taking place, and it was impossible to ignore Brandon's freeze-out and silent treatment. Needless to say, whenever our paths did cross, all eyes were fixed, and the closest encounter of the Brandon-and-Darcy kind took place when Irv had us practice covering steals of second base.

Defensing the slide is a fundamental play; however, it is one of the most frequently botched. Irv wants us to straddle the bag (as opposed to standing in front of it) and to place our tags with one hand. He wants us to wait for the throw with our gloves hovering between our knees. He doesn't want us reaching for the ball (except for short throws) because then you have to reach back for the runner, which is usually the difference between a steal and a caught-stealing.

But no one really cared about those finer points except for me. Everyone else—including the pretty boy himself—was too preoccupied with whether Brandon and I would come to blows since Irv insisted that Brandon be the runner and I be the tagger.

Each time I took the throw, I got to tag Brandon, and as luck would have it, every throw from the catcher was absolutely perfect. So I got to tag him hard. On the shoulder. On the chest. On the head. On the leg. And each time I tagged his leg, I made sure I smacked the exact same spot.

After about tag-twelve, Brandon had had all that he could handle. He jumped to his feet and into baseball-fight ready-position.

Now most baseball fights aren't exactly fights. They're nothing more than individuals cursing in each other's faces with their chests expanded and their arms at their sides. Occasionally, there will be an exchange of shoves, and on the extremely rare occasion an actual punch will be thrown (it's a virtual given that it misses).

But I simply backed away from Brandon. I wanted no part of this.

Plus did he really truly believe we were going to exchange blows? C'mon, let's be realistic here. Yeah, it's a thin line between love and hate, but this was taking things to an absurd extreme.

And there was another, more important reason why I wanted no part of this pseudo-altercation. That was, with each passing play and each passing drill, it was becoming more and more apparent that Irv was looking to me to be the team's leader. Irv wanted *me* taking charge. He wanted everyone looking at me, watching my example.

So cool.

Still I did manage to have some fun at Brandon's expense. Did you really think I wouldn't? It happened a short time later, when Irv had us practice the double play.

"Next ten minutes, we get two on every groundball!" Irv stood at home plate and pointed his bat at his fielders.

Of course, once again I was that same, sugared-up seven-year-old, and I'm sure the fact that I turn the double play better than anyone had something to do with my overflowing ebullience.

For me the key to the double play is driving off the outfield side of the bag instead of coming across it. I'm able to do this since we have immovable bases in our conference, and the immovable base acts as protection against any six-foot-two, two-hundred-twelve-pound runner who's bearing down on me thinking he can intimidate the chick. Of course, the fact that I have a strong and accurate throwing arm that I'm not afraid to use doesn't hurt matters either. If that runner decides to stay in the path of my throw, he will be learning close up the laws of physics and motion.

Now last year Sam and Brandon were the team's double play combination, but this year . . . well, this year Brandon was rotating in on every fourth groundball.

Ouch!

When Sam and I practice turning dps, we have a blast because on a baseball level, we have gelled. We have perfect timing and absolute confidence in the other's ability. On top of that we are nonstop chatter. Translation: Not only does Brandon have to endure watching us flawlessly turn double play after double play; he also has to put up with our endless banter.

"Just get your throws close," I called to Sam across the infield. "Keep 'em above the waist, and I'll take care of the rest."

"Keep 'em above the waist? That's what Sam always tells me."

"Right! No way is my Samantha telling any boy to keep anything above the waist!"

Sam laughed. "You mind if I throw my balls in hard?"

"Don't mind at all, as long as you're not on top of me."

Brandon tried to ignore this. Like he had a chance in hell. He couldn't mask his feelings or his poor play. On consecutive chances, he juggled a flip from Sam and then threw his relay throw into the bleachers behind first.

"Get your act together, Brandon!" Irv yelled. "You field like that, you won't even be out there when Darcy's pitching."

Double ouch!

Without a doubt and to put it mildly, baseball had gone from Brandon's amusement park to his abusement park.

And at this point I needed some big-time advice.

24

"Sam, we need to talk."

Say those five words to Samantha and she just about loses it (which assumes she hasn't already lost it) because it means Sam gets to play therapist, and there's nothing Sam loves more, except maybe shopping, gossiping, shopping, chatting online, shopping, talking on her cells (yes, plural), shopping . . .

But the thing is, as much as Sam loves to play therapist, she isn't very good at it (surprise, surprise). She's kinda like a Jekyll-and-Hyde therapist. Sometimes she's real good, nodding and uh-huhing at appropriate times, and after she's collected enough data, she formulates a solid opinion and offers healthy advice. But other times she can't listen to a word you're saying, not even if you're talking about her (I know, difficult to believe).

Like she always does when Sam gets to play Doctor Feel Good, she led me to the sensory-deprivation room in her house.

I kid you not.

A couple years ago, Sam's parents built themselves a sound-proof-lightproof relaxation room, kinda like a 1950s bomb shelter, only it's aboveground and furnished with funky chairs and couches supposedly designed to perfectly fit the contours of the human body. I had never heard of such a thing and simply assumed it was either an LA thing, since that's where her mom was originally from, or a Nepal thing, since her dad visited there on business and they had the room built immediately upon his return.

Josh theorized otherwise (another surprise, surprise). He said the room was a QVC impulse purchase, payable in twenty-four low monthly payments of $89.95, with the furnishings being the "if you act now, we'll also throw in these beautiful . . ." component of the purchase. Alternatively, he believed the room was the product of an online-auction bidding war gone awry.

"I don't know what to do about Brandon," I began.

Sam popped a bubble. "What's there to do?"

We were lying on parallel couches a few feet apart in the pitch dark.

"He's so pissed he won't even acknowledge my presence."

"This surprises you? What planet do you live on? And what happened to your pathetic no-fly zone anyway?"

"I didn't think he'd keep it up for this long."

"Miller, what's with you?" Sam popped another bubble. "You told me you're glad he's ignoring you. It's allowing you to focus on the team and concentrate your efforts. As a matter of fact, that's exactly what you said online last night and the night before that. I still have the IMs."

I clasped my hands behind my neck. "Y'know before our parents started dating, Brandon and I always had this thing and—"

"Miller, I need to interrupt."

"What?" I growled.

"I know you require my therapeutic expertise, but do we really need to relive the past?" She cracked her knuckles. "It's bad enough I had to go through this with you once. I really don't think it's necessary to go through it again."

"Brandon and I . . . have always had this thing, but as soon as our parents started dating, the situation . . . it all became so humiliating. We couldn't—"

"Oh, and one more thing."

"*What?*"

"When you finally decide to fast forward to the good parts, spare me the all-I-want-is-to-play-for-the-baseball-team bullshit. That's so six weeks ago."

"Can I continue?"

"Of course, hon."

"Oh, thanks." I blew the hair off my face and shut my eyes. Sam's incessant interruptions made it painfully obvious that today's "therapy" installment was going to be fruitless.

Longdeeplongdeeplongdeep breath.

"With all that's happened over these last few weeks and months, I look at Brandon so differently now."

"Uh-huh."

"He's like . . . it's like I'm dealing with a whole other person."

"Uh-huh."

"I mean, until now no matter . . . no matter how I felt for him, I couldn't see past that he was the principal's son."

"Uh-huh."

"No matter how cool he was, or how good an athlete he was, or ohmigod, how cute he looked in his OshKosh overalls."

"Uh-huh."

Hold the phone.

My last comment should've elicited much more than a blasé "uh-huh." Bitch-Sam was yessing me!

I sat up.

"Josh and I had sex six times last night."

"Uh-huh."

"Sam!" I whine-screamed.

"What?" she whine-screamed back even louder and more annoyingly.

"I just said I had sex with Josh six times!"

"I heard you the first time!"

"*Josh!*" I screamed. "I said Josh! And all you said was 'uh-huh.'"

Sam cracked her gum. "Miller, you were testing me to see if I was listening. What do you want me to say?"

I wanted to shake her.

Longdeeplongdeeplongdeep breath.

"Sam, Brandon is so . . . he's almost perfect. The way he looks in those muscle tees when he's all sweaty after practice, and the way he wears his cap backward, and when he plays, he's so hot, and he's such a good athlete, and when . . . he didn't choose to be the principal's son."

"Are you defending him or telling me?"

"Brandon's nothing like his father, Sam. It has to be one of the great unsolved mysteries of humankind how two such strikingly different people can come from a common gene pool."

"Why are you telling me this?"

"We're together on the baseball field almost two hours a day, and for a good part of that time we're side by side, rotating through drills—"

"Miller, it's so clear what's happening. I'm surprised even you weren't able to figure this one out. He's gonna ask you out."

"What?"

"He's gonna ask you out. Watch."

"Shut up."

"No doubt in my mind."

"Sam, he's not even speaking to me. How's he gonna ask me out?"

"I guarantee it."

"No way."

"Miller, no matter what pathetic dance you two have been engaging in for everyone to see, I bet he's been watching and keeping tabs on you as much as you've been watching and keeping tabs on him. Every time you've been spying on him—"

"I'm not spying on him."

"Miller, you're watching him, and you don't want him to see you. Sounds like spying to me."

"I'm not spying on him," I repeated.

"Miller, here's a question for you: Have you caught *him* looking at *you*?"

An "I'm screwed" question if I ever heard one. If I said yes, it proved her point, which is the last thing you ever want to do, and if I said no, I was . . .

"I think I have," I replied softly. "I'm not sure."

Sam popped a bubble. "Miller, if you think you've seen him looking at you, you have. It's called flirting."

"He's not flirting."

"Three days," Sam said.

"What's three days?"

"Three days max. Three days till he asks you out."

I wanted to shake her. "Shut up, Sam." She was working my last nerve.

"Wanna bet?"

25

Let's just say I'm glad I didn't accept Sam's bet because at practice the next day Brandon came up to me as soon as we started fielding practice.

"So what's your take on it?" he asked.

"He can talk!" I wished the lame words back as they rolled off my lips.

"Very funny, Darcy."

"Why are you speaking to me all of a sudden?"

"I asked you a question."

He had, hadn't he? I was so surprised he had spoken to me, I couldn't remember what he'd asked.

Okay, this was weird. Even weird for Brandon and me. I recognized he was trying to break the ice, but this? A nonsensical, open-ended, out-of-the-blue question? Even from a super-deflated Brandon Basset, I expected something else (although truthfully, I hadn't really been expecting anything).

"I don't know," I guessed.

"C'mon, Darcy. What do you mean you don't know? You have to have an opinion."

I shuddered.

Suddenly I had this déjà vu feeling of being in Principal Basset's office all over again. Brandon was talking about something, and I had no idea what, only I was expected to know; therefore, if I asked the right question or gave the right response, there was a chance I could figure out what the hell he was talking about.

Maybe this ran in the family. Maybe it was a Basset family trait to initiate conversation by speaking in riddles.

"I don't really have an opinion," I shrugged.

"Bullshit, Darcy. Like hell you don't. What's your take on them?"

"*Them who?*" I couldn't play this game again. I needed to know what we were talking about.

"Our parents!"

"How the hell was I supposed to know you were talking about our parents?"

"Who else would I be talking about?"

"Well, gee, Brandon, let's see. You haven't spoken to me in a week, and then out of nowhere you come up to me and start talking again. I'm to guess you're talking about our parents?"

I shuddered again.

Talk about places I never thought I'd be. Here I was standing in the middle of varsity baseball practice discussing the current state of my mom's relationship with my principal—with said principal's son!

Something was up. Something had to be up. Why was Brandon suddenly breaking the ice right here and now and like this?

Instantly (instinctively?) thoughts turned to Josh.

Josh.

Josh had done something. Had Josh done something? The regular season opener was only three days away, so he needed to act soon (although knowing the season began in three days would require Josh to understand the concept of a baseball schedule).

Was I reading way too much into all this?

Maybe Brandon was simply tired of this whole silent-treatment charade. Maybe it was bothering him more than it was bothering me. Maybe he had resolved it in his mind that he was somehow "letting" me play shortstop. Maybe he felt that enough was enough. Maybe since our lone preseason game was tomorrow, it was time to reopen the lines of communication because . . .

No.

Brandon was about to ask me out. Holy shit, Brandon was going to ask me out. Right here and now.

Sam was right.

I was more numb than I had been in the student lounge after Principal Braindead informed me I was a lesbian.

"You're up," Brandon said.

I didn't react. Stuck in a state of suspended disbelief.

"I said you're up." He motioned for me to take the next ground-ball.

I still couldn't react.

"Okay"—he stepped around me, smiling mischievously—"I'll take it."

As he fielded *my* round of grounders, my motor skills slowly returned, but at this same time I was also blessed with a visit from Sam's voice.

"Three days max. Three days till he asks you out."

"Am I making you uncomfortable?" Brandon walked back over after his last ball. His smug smile hadn't left his face.

"Not at all," I (rep)lied.

"So then what's your take on it?" he pressed.

"I don't want to talk about it here."

"So I am making you uncomfortable."

"No, you're not."

"We going to argue about this, too?"

"Looks that way."

Brandon was back to his old cocky self. It was frightening how quickly he had returned from the land of the mute.

"They're going away together," he stated matter-of-factly.

"In a few weeks."

Irv was motioning with his bat that the next set of grounders was coming our way.

"You're up." Brandon motioned with his glove.

Irv grounded four straight rocket one-hoppers to me. I fielded each one effortlessly (as usual).

"Nice job," Brandon said. He held out his glove to be high-fived.

I stared at the glove and then at him.

First he was talking to me, and now he was complimenting me. This was getting freaky.

No matter the case I couldn't leave him hanging. It would be bad form under any circumstances. I tapped his glove.

"You go to your right better than I do," he said.

Okay, things were no longer *getting* freaky. Things *were* freaky.

In a matter of seconds, Brandon had covered the entire spectrum, from PMS-induced, silent-treatment freeze-out all the way to gregarious conversation and ego-stroking compliments.

"Three days max. Three days till he asks you out."

Sam's voice again.

The hunch was stronger than ever.

God, I hated it when she was right. He was going to do it. Right here and now in the middle of practice.

But he didn't. Not even when we held eye contact that extra split second at the end of fielding drills.

He didn't. Sam had been wrong. And I *knew* she was right. Even though I told her to shut up, I had been positive too. But no.

Wow.

Damn.

Something was up. Something *had* to be up.

26

We were all set to have our one and only exhibition game against Creggan North, and Irv was going to have Specs, Reynaldo, and me each throw two or three innings since none of us had faced live batters or seen any competition outside of intrasquad games. Needless to say, there couldn't have been a straitjacket strong enough to contain even a portion of my pumped-up person, but . . .

The game was canceled because of rain.

Well, not exactly because of rain. Sure it rained a little in the morning, but the sun had been out all afternoon, and . . .

Allow me to explain: Creggan's coach and Irv don't like each other. *Really* don't like each other. They constantly engage in grade-school gamesmanship whose sole purpose is to annoy the hell out of each other. They usually succeed. Last year it even resulted in a home plate shoving match during the pregame exchange of lineup cards.

On the day of the exhibition game, Creggan's coach called forty-five minutes before game time to inform us they weren't coming. Their athletic department had received several phone calls claiming our field was too wet, and that rain was still in the forecast. The fact that Irv assured them (by swearing on the graves of his players) that our field was bone-dry, that he was staring at the

Doppler radar on this computer at this moment, and that there wasn't a cloud in the sky for three counties in every direction was of no consequence.

But . . .

And this is the bigger but . . .

I was responsible for the misinformation. Yes, me.

Why would I do such a thing? Why would I sabotage my own dream?

One word: Josh. Josh was going to attack. Today. At the game.

Now it was only a hunch, and I know my recent track record on hunches wasn't exactly . . . well, this time I wasn't wrong. This hunch was much more like the ones associated with Josh when we're mutually attracted to a boy. I felt this one in my bones.

So I masterminded the cancellation of our one-game exhibition season.

Hey, drastic times call for drastic measures.

God, I had wanted to play. This was going to be my only chance to play against another team, to face other batters before playing the Danforth Dragons in the opener. No, it wouldn't have been the same as a regular season game, but it would have been the closest I had come (so far) to fulfilling my baseball dream.

Playing was also going to take my mind off the Brandon situation. The fact that he hadn't asked me out had left me so insanely perplexed that I even considered asking *him* out.

I could, you know. I mean, let's face it, there are some extremely peculiar dynamics at work here, and it's not required that we defer to typical gender roles defined by teen magazines and reality TV. Sure, Brandon should be the one doing the asking, but if we were to look at things in baseball terms (which is not completely irrational in light of the circumstances), then *I* should be the one calling the

shots. On top of that, you can't discount the whole falsehood fac-
tor: I'm a lesbian, and no guy in his right mind is going to ask out
a lesbian. Talk about begging to be Heisman-ed!

But Brandon knows my predicament. Hell, he created it! He
should just do the normal guy thing.

"I can't believe we're not playing," I finally said to Specs and
Reynaldo. The three of us were standing along the first base line
looking out at the field, which except for a lone rakeable puddle
near shortstop was as dry as a desert.

"Tell me about it," Reynaldo said. "Irv's gonna shit. He hates
rainouts."

"Especially when it's not raining," Specs added. "He's gonna put
us through hell."

I smiled. "I guess this is what you'd call a premature cancellation!"

We all laughed.

But the laughing stopped when Irv reached the field and gathered the team around the mound. It was as clear as this day that
Reynaldo and Specs were right. Irv couldn't wait to burst a vessel,
and in order to achieve that end, he decided to devote the entire
ninety-minute practice to situations, which meant that something
was going to set him off. It was just a question of what.

Yes, Irv was setting us up. Coaches do that from time to time.
It's a coaching technique, a way of keeping players sharp and focus-
ing their minds and lighting a fire and combating complacency
and creating a hunger and spurring a drive and . . . you know, all
those other buzzwords and clichés coaches regurgitate. Irv had
detected the not-in-the-mood-for-practice feeling among his players, and that, coupled with his pissy mood, were the ingredients
and recipe for disaster.

Now if there had been one area Irv had neglected during practices (and I'm not saying there was), it had been simulating game scenarios. So as we jogged out to our positions, I sensed this could get ugly in a hurry.

"Base hit right field, runners on first and second!" Irv stood by home plate and called out to the players on the field.

Irv grounded a ball into right. I set up for the cutoff throw to third, Sam broke to second, and the rightfielder fielded the ball cleanly. But the centerfielder didn't move over to help out in right, and Specs didn't break from the mound toward the third base line to back up the throw.

"What was that?" Irv leaned disgustedly on his fungo bat. "Everyone needs to be thinking! Why aren't we talking out here?" He ordered us back to our positions, inserting Reynaldo for Specs. "Let's try it again. Nobody on, extra-base hit to the gap in left center."

WE INTERRUPT PRACTICE FOR A SPECIAL BULLETIN:
JOSH ALERT!
JOSH HAS BEEN SPOTTED IN THE VICINITY!

Holy shit! This was it!

Josh had driven his car right up onto the makeshift bullpen mounds beyond the Dumpsters behind third base, a privilege and area reserved for school maintenance vehicles and clandestine drug transactions. The backseat of his SUV was packed (explosives?) and from my distant vantage point, I was able to see cartons, signs, and Mylar balloons, but I knew there was so much more.

This was no exercise. No military fly-by. This was the real deal.

Suddenly, the driver's-side door swung open and Josh emerged. Slowly he walked around the front of the still-idling vehicle. He stared out at the field, shading his eyes from the blinding sunshine.

Even from this distance, I could tell he was puzzled and confused.

Yes! My preemptive strike had worked! I had avoided thermonuclear Armageddon . . . for now.

Ping!

The sound of ball-meeting-aluminum brought me back. Irv's perfectly placed frozen rope into the right centerfield gap resulted in a different (but equally lethal) form of hell breaking loose.

The leftfielder failed to break in, the first baseman didn't pretend to trail the baserunner circling the bases, and—what I know pissed Irv off most—Sam failed to line up properly for the cutoff throw.

When an infielder lines up for a relay throw, he (she) must have what I call *Exorcist* head, the ability to swivel one's head in all directions so he (she) can simultaneously see his (her) outfielders and pick up the runners behind him (her) so that he (she) will know where the ball should go once he (she) receives the throw. In addition, an outfielder does not throw *to* the cutoff (wo)man. He (she) throws *through* the cutoff (wo)man. A cutoff (wo)man is either cutting it or letting it go through to the relay (wo)man. The ideal position for this cutoff (wo)man is the shallowest point where the outfielder can hit him (her) on the fly, or the deepest point where the cutoff (wo)man can make a strong throw that takes no more than one hop to its destination. The relay (wo)man is the infielder who puts him(her)self in position to make the ultimate throw.

Got all that? Well, we didn't.

And, oh, by the way, not only did we totally screw up the everybody-needs-to-be-thinking part, but we also royally hosed the why-aren't-we-talking-out-here part, too. There wasn't a single "Cut

Phil Bildner

throw" or "Let it go" or "Plate! Plate!" from any of us.

Irv ordered the entire team to the mound.

"What the hell are you guys doing out there?" he shouted, picking up the rosin bag and launching it into left field. "And I say *guys* because the only one who seems to have any sense out there is Darcy!"

I was trying to maintain eye contact with Irv while still monitoring Josh, who was apparently retreating back to his vehicle. It was next to impossible to focus on both, and as a result the full extent of Irv's statements wasn't registering.

Irv now directed his wrath at Sam.

"When Darcy's at short, she's in charge of that infield. You got that?"

Sam nodded meekly.

"You defer to her. I want someone who knows what the hell is going on out there making the decisions. You got that?"

He nodded meekly again.

The full extent of Irv's words was definitely registering now. This was a public coronation. Irv wanted *me* calling the shots.

Me, Darcy Miller.

I had just become the official leader of the Finley Force varsity boys' baseball team. And at the very moment we had skirted the apocalypse. This was definitely some kind of sign.

So cool.

27

Brandon was waiting for me by my car after practice, standing in front of the driver's side door. I immediately had flashbacks of Josh from a few days ago.

"Congratulations, captain," he said.

"What are you talking about?" I knew exactly what he was talking about.

"Irv just named you captain."

"No, he didn't. That was an Irv hissy fit."

"No, you were just captained."

"I don't think so." I held firm, even though I couldn't agree with him more. I hopped onto the hood and began picking the mud from my cleats with a Popsicle stick.

"So what are you doing Saturday night?"

Boom!

Finally! He was asking me out . . . sorta.

"I don't know, why?"

He sat down beside me. "Just curious." He gave me his head tilt and smile.

"You asking me out?"

"Depends."

"Depends on . . . no, I'm not playing this game."

"What game?" Brandon still smiled.

"The game where you sorta ask me out so if I say yes, you did ask me out, but if I say no, you never asked me anything."

"I don't play that game." Brandon's smile was now a full-fledged grin.

"You invented it, right?"

"Something like that." Brandon ran his hand over his mouth like he was figuratively and literally wiping away his smile.

I wanted to melt. In fact, I felt myself starting to wobble, and I know Brandon must have seen it too because at the exact same moment I reached for him, he reached for me, and then . . .

It happened. Something just clicked. Simultaneously. Yes. For both of us. It happened.

And just like that, it was game over. Just like that, our posturing contest was done, and like two exhausted pugilists, it was finally time for us to lay down our gloves.

"Darcy, would you like to do something with me Saturday night?" Brandon asked. He held my fingers, and the rush through my blood and veins felt like he had given me a bear hug.

I smiled. A smile of relief. A smile of joy.

Brandon smiled back.

"Yeah, Brandon, I'd like to do something with you."

"Cool."

"This is going to be interesting," I said when I was finally able to breathe again.

"I'll say!" He wove his fingers into mine.

"We have to be discreet."

"That shouldn't be a problem." Brandon laughed. "You are a lesbian, you know."

His words surprised me. Maybe that was another reason why

Brandon had told his father what he did. If his father thought I was a lesbian—if everyone thought I was a lesbian—then it wouldn't matter if Brandon and I hung out together. No one would suspect a thing, and if that was the case, we'd be able to date.

Snap out of it, Darcy!

Here I was having my long-awaited and overdue romantic and tender moment with the boy of my dreams, and I was overanalyzing matters that no longer mattered.

"I have to tell Samantha." I bit my lower lip and turned away.

"Samantha! That's like attaching a banner to the back of a plane!"

"She'll be cool. Trust me. I've got too much dirt on her."

"If you say so."

"I say so." I placed our hands atop his leg. "I'm more concerned about Josh. Did you see him at practice?"

"Don't worry about it."

"Don't worry about it? He was about to drive onto the field with a car full of—"

"I'm tellin' ya, fuhgeddaboudit."

"It's kinda hard to forget about it."

Brandon squeezed my hand. "You've got nothing to worry about."

"It's not just me I'm worried about. We only dodged that bullet today because the game was cancelled, which it never should have been. But that's a whole other story." I muttered the last clause almost inaudibly.

"Yo, I'm tellin' ya, fuhgeddaboudit."

"Stop joking. We *can't* forget about this."

"It'll all work out, Darcy. Trust me on this. I'm gonna take care of it." He let go of my hand so that he could touch my face like he had during our moment in the boys' bathroom.

"Brandon, you don't understand, it's—"

"Shhh," he placed a finger over my lips. Then he leaned in and kissed me, the most perfect, gentle, softest kiss I ever felt.

And when he finished and started to move away, I wished he never would, and like in a Lifetime TV movie, my wish momentarily came true, for he kissed me again, an even more perfect, gentler, softer kiss than his first.

"I like this." Brandon was beaming. His hand rested against my cheek.

I felt so safe. So safe that I wanted to tell him every last fear and worry about Josh, but I was too overcome to even form words.

"I have a confession to make." His fingers tucked some strands of hair behind my hair. He still beamed.

"Am I . . . am I going to like this?" I managed to ask.

Brandon's warm smile answered my question. "There's another reason why I wanted you to play baseball." He ran his fingers over my lips again. "It was . . . with our parents going out and all . . . I needed to find a way to get close to you again."

I wanted to melt. Again. Forever.

"This was my chance."

"Wow," I whispered. I didn't know what else to say. I didn't know if there was anything I could say.

"I like this," Brandon said again.

He leaned in again, and even though I didn't think it was possible, he kissed me an even more perfect, gentle, and soft kiss. More perfect than the first two. Combined.

And despite all my underlying horrific fears, I liked this too.

A lot.

28

"I told ya!"

Samantha was screaming so loud I had to hold my cell at arm's length.

"You need to calm down, Sam. Discretion, remember?"

"I knew it, Miller. I told ya."

"This is under the radar, Sam. Do you hear me?"

"I told ya!"

"Tell me 'I told ya' one more time and I'm hanging up."

I was stuck in traffic on the way home from practice, so I wasn't exactly in a Sam 'I told ya' frame of mind.

"What did he say? How did he do it?" she asked.

"He asked me after practice."

"And what did you say?"

"I said yes. Keep your voice down."

"No, Miller, exactly what did you say? Did you say 'yes,' or 'yeah,' or 'okay,' or 'maybe,' or 'I don't want to date, I just want to fool around'?"

"That last one. I told him I wanted to be just like you."

"Don't be a bitch, Miller. So when are you going out?"

"This weekend."

"Well, if he suggests Friday, tell him you can only go out

Saturday. Whatever day he suggests, say you have plans with me."

"Why would I do that?"

"You're in the game now, Miller. You gotta play."

"What is it with everyone and playing games?"

"Games are a part of it."

"You got that, girlfriend!" a third voice added. "Games are always a part of it!"

"Who said that?" I asked angrily.

"It's just the woman sitting next to me."

"You're at the spa?"

"Where else would I be?"

Good god! Sam was talking to me while she was getting her toes done.

"Sam, I'm not even going to try to play your games because I can't even begin to understand the rules!"

"Well, Miller, let me tell you something, you *need* to understand, because when you've played by your inept rules, the closest thing you've gotten to getting any is . . . is with Josh." She laughed. "What are you guys gonna do? Where you gonna go? I know this fabulous—"

"He said he'd call me." I cut her off.

"When?"

"I don't know. Whenever."

"Like tonight? Or tomorrow after school? Or tomorrow night?"

"How should I know? And can you please lower your voice?"

"Oh, Miller," Sam groaned, "you need so much work. But you do know what this means, don't you?"

"It's time for me to hang up on you?"

"I'll pretend you didn't say that." Sam cleared her throat. "Let me try again. You do know what this means, don't you?"

"Let me guess. You're about to explain, and I have to listen, right?"

There was a short pause. "Miller, I'll ask you one last time. You do know what this means, don't you?"

"No," I answered obediently.

"Miller, the potentials are limitless. We can finally double-date. We can go to the prom together. We can all do beach weekends."

Sam has a very different concept of the term "discreet."

"I don't know, Sam."

"Sure you do. It'll be great."

"Sam, Brandon and I can't let anyone know. We have to be low-key. Very low-key."

"I can do low-key."

"Puh-lease."

The girl's on the phone with me in the middle of a pedicure with six women sitting around her, each one hanging onto every last syllable rolling off her lips, and she's telling me she can do low-key. Next thing she'll be telling me she's low-maintenance and does volunteer work.

"So what does your *other* boyfriend have to say about this latest development?"

I paused. "I haven't told him yet."

"Ooh! The plot thickens again."

"Tell me about it. I'm a dead dyke!"

Sam laughed. "That's one way of putting it."

"If he ruins this for me, I'll never forgive him. Never."

"Miller, the boy is evil. I've always told you that. It's only a matter of time before he does."

"Don't remind me. I've played out every scenario trying to figure out the wheres, whens, and hows. Would you believe he showed up at practice today? The time was—"

"Speaking of time, Miller, I'm just about done here, and I need to get an outfit for tomorrow. Wanna meet me?"

"What's tomorrow?"

"The meeting."

"What meeting?" I asked nervously.

"The GSA meeting."

I immediately pulled over to the shoulder. It was no longer safe to drive with Sam feeding me information like this.

"Sam, why are *you* going to GSA?"

"Miller, I wouldn't miss this for a Shoshanna sample sale! This is gonna be historic. With all that's going on between you and Brandon, and with this once-in-a-lifetime opportunity to drive Josh crazy, and—"

"Sam, as a friend, I'm asking you . . . no, I'm begging you, whatever you do, please don't—"

"Miller," Sam interrupted me with several cracks of gum, "don't even *think* of telling me not to come."

29

Josh needed to hear about this from me. Even though he was plotting to go medieval on me and all those around me, I still felt it was my duty to inform him of this latest development.

Unfortunately, I didn't get to him until ten minutes before GSA, and my timing couldn't have been worse. He was mid-panic attack, having just dropped his Egg McMuffin on the V-neck sweater he had purchased special for today's meeting.

Yes, for the GSA president, regularly scheduled meetings doubled as fashion events, and the fact that he was now forced to wear a Miami Heat XXL T-shirt he had borrowed from some sophomore was a sure sign of something.

The Miami Heat? Josh? Knowing Josh, he probably thought he was wearing a giveaway courtesy of the Weather Channel.

Still, despite his frantic and fragile state, I couldn't allow him to just walk in on a Sam-attended GSA meeting. The earth's axis isn't *that* strong.

"Josh, I need to tell you something."

"BSB, go die in a minute."

"I have to tell you something."

"Do you not have eyes?" Josh's ears began to redden. "Now's not a good time."

"It's important."

"*What?* What is so important that you have to tell me right now?"

We had been standing in the hallway outside the side entrance to the student lounge, hardly a private setting. So I took him by the arm to a place I was now quite familiar with—the boys' bathroom—and just like I had with Brandon a couple weeks ago, I strategically placed him away from the door.

I opted to ease into my piece of really bad news with a piece of ordinary bad news.

"Brandon asked me out, and I said yes."

Josh opened his mouth to yell, scream, or spontaneously combust, but I didn't give him the chance.

"You need to listen."

"Go to hell!" he yelled, pointing in my face.

"You need to listen."

"No! Don't you dare tell me what I need to do!"

Josh was beginning to bug. Clearly it had been a wise decision to relocate to the rest room.

"Fine, then will you listen?"

"No, I won't listen. I have a meeting to go to." He looked at his watch. "Or should I say *we* have a meeting to go to, you freakin' fake. You and your boyfriend—"

"Keep your voice down!"

He was screaming so loud I knew peeps could hear him in the hall.

"No, I won't keep my voice down! It's about time people knew the truth!"

"Josh! Stop!"

"You're having a real good time with all this, aren't you, BSB?"

"Josh, please." I went for the soft approach and touched his arm.

"No! This ride's about to end. This roller coaster's about to jump the tracks."

"Josh, I know you're upset, but I wish—"

"Upset? Of course I'm upset! I had dibs!"

"Dibs?" I busted out laughing. "Dibs? Oh, *puh-lease*, Josh."

Josh was mortified. "Dibs" was the last thing he had wanted to emerge from his mouth, but sometimes he gets so riled, the words just come out on their own.

Unfiltered.

Suddenly I no longer needed to go with the arm-touching, gentle approach. In fact, I no longer needed to go with any preplanned or well thought out approach. No, I now had the upper hand, the ability to turn the tables on this conversation and throw everything right back in *his* face. And even though I knew better, I couldn't resist such an opportunity. Moments like these were rarities.

"Joshy boy, we're not fighting over who gets the top bunk or who gets to ride shotgun. I'm not your little brother."

"BSB, I liked him first."

"Oh, there's another mature argument. Like that was going to make a difference?"

Josh was digging himself quite a hole. Perhaps he thought the way to extract himself was to go even deeper.

"'I liked him first,'" I mocked.

Josh didn't respond. And I didn't relent. "Josh, just because you have some Marcia *Brady Bunch*, puppy-love crush on out-of-your-league, straight-boy Brandon Basset, he's not allowed to like or date anyone else? That makes a lot of sense."

Slam!

Even I felt the sting of that zinger.

"Of all the guys at Finley, the one you have to choose is . . ." Josh was shaking his head and fighting a pre-cry frown. "Just remember, BSB, what goes around, comes around. And yours is en route."

He started to storm off, but I grabbed his arm as he brushed by. "There's more, Josh."

He glared through tearing eyes.

"There's one more thing you need to know."

"What?"

Longdeeplongdeeplongdeep breath.

"Sam's gonna be at GSA."

30

"First of all, I'd like to thank everyone for coming." Josh stood in front of Mr. Bitner's standing-room-only classroom sporting his red and black, dress-length Miami Heat tee. "This is by far the largest turnout we've ever had for GSA. I'm actually a little nervous speaking to so many people. Now before we officially get down to business, I'd like to say something."

Uh-oh.

I looked over at Brandon sitting on the windowsill next to Leslie White. He motioned with his hands for me to remain calm.

Fat chance.

Josh walked around Mr. Bitner's desk and sat down on the front of it. Josh is an excellent public speaker, and I recognized his tactical move. He was removing the desk as a partition, eliminating the barrier between himself and his audience.

This was it.

"It's nice to see this many people here. I'm genuinely touched. It makes me feel very good knowing we've created something so special in such a short time. Still, a part of me remains skeptical. I guess that's my nature. Growing up gay, you're naturally a little less trusting, a little more hesitant. You go about things a little more cautiously than you would if you were straight because . . . because you have to."

The optional attendance sheet reached my desk, but for the moment I was too focused on Josh to sign my name and pass it along.

"It's important that people come to GSA for the right reasons. Don't get me wrong. It goes without saying we'd love to have everyone's support. That would be incredible, and it would be far beyond anything I ever envisioned." Josh paused for a sip from his diet Dr Pepper. "But something needs to be understood, and it's difficult to articulate this without sounding harsh. GSA is a different type of school organization. We demand that our members demonstrate a level of commitment far greater than what might be expected at other Finley clubs, groups, or organizations. Now what exactly does that mean?"

I signed the attendance sheet and started passing it to the person to my right, but I caught myself. The person to my right happened to be Sam. Bad idea. I was trying to completely ignore her. I didn't want to have any interaction with her at all. Absolutely no good could come of it. Plus I could tell Sam didn't want to be disturbed because she was busy arranging her bottles of nail polish and base, cotton balls, and paper towels. I leaned forward, passed the attendance form back to the person who had given it to me, and pointed it off in another direction.

"We require our members to demonstrate their commitment through activism," Josh continued. "Activism can mean a number of things, but in all instances it means giving your time and putting in an amount of work that some people . . . that some people may find excessive." He stood up. "But there's a reason we do this. A person who does satisfy this criteria is interested in furthering the interests of GSA. But looking around this room today, I have to say, I know many of you are not willing to make that commitment. I know it. I do. I'm not saying that to be rude. I'm saying that because I'm a realist. I'm saying it from experience. I know."

In Josh's defense, I understood what he was saying. It's frustrating leading a school organization where fifty-four people show up for one or two meetings, but five or six end up doing all the work.

Josh looked around the room and allowed his gaze to zoom in on a few people. Of course, Brandon, Sam, and I were all high-profile targets.

"There are people here today for the wrong reasons." He now spoke with more of an edge. "For these people, GSA is nothing more than an opportunity to pad a resumé, to create college interview fodder, or as is the case today, to satisfy an agenda."

I looked over at Brandon and Leslie again. He was chewing hard on his lower lip. She was glaring evil.

I looked over at Gilberto, standing by the door with his arms crossed, nodding along with every last word coming from Josh's mouth. Mr. Bitner stood beside him, reading his paperback and paying little mind to the words being spoken. I then allowed myself a quick peek at Sam. I wanted to shake the satanic smile from her face.

Can you say powder keg?

"There are two people here today," Josh went on, "who need to be addressed directly because—"

"May I say something?"

Every head turned in the direction of the voice.

Brandon.

I spun back to Josh. He had a look of horror like he had just learned his Abercrombie & Fitch spring break catalog was lost in the mail.

"No, you can't," Josh snapped. "I'm speaking, and as a matter of fact—"

Phil Bildner

"Well, with all due respect," Brandon interrupted again, "I'd like to say something *now* because your comments are directed at me."

"Yes, my comments are directed at you, but no, you still can't say something."

I slid down in my seat and peeked at Sam. Utter glee was plastered on her face.

"This is only my second meeting," Brandon persisted, "and I'm confused by the mixed messages—"

"Brandon, you need to wait. If you like, you can speak when we open the floor, but GSA isn't like a halftime meeting at one of your baseball games. This isn't a free-for-all where you speak when you see fit."

Brandon sighed. "I'll say it again—"

"No, you won't. You need to be quiet, or you need to leave."

I slumped down even farther.

"Excuse me, Josh." Leslie White hopped off the windowsill. "Brandon's right. Your opening remarks were aimed squarely at him. It's only fair he gets to respond."

"He can respond," Josh answered, "but not right now."

"Well I, for one, would like to hear what he has to say now."

A smattering of students clapped.

"Leslie, I think you're out of line," came a voice from the other side of the room.

Uh-oh.

Gilberto had unfolded his arms and stepped forward.

"Who asked you?" Leslie growled back.

"Who asked you?" Gilberto replied.

We had ignition!

Bedlam. Chaos. Disaster!

I slid as low as I could in my seat and ducked my head, but regrettably I glanced toward Sam again, who was clapping her hands and stamping her feet like a child at the circus.

"This is exactly why we don't open the floor!" Josh leaped onto Mr. Bitner's desk. "This is why we don't let people speak out simply when they want to!" He jumped up and down, his arms extended upward and outward, waving about.

Amazingly his crazed attention-getting ploy worked. In an instant all eyes had refocused on him.

"Listen, when we started this GSA chapter, we promised *this* would never happen." He spoke from atop the desk. "A lack of order and a lack of decorum lead to nothing. Literally nothing. Nothing gets accomplished. That happens at practically every club in this high school, and there's no way GSA wants to be just like every other Finley club." He jumped down. "We're not every other club. At GSA, I can proudly say, at every meeting we've ever held—every meeting—we've always accomplished tangible ends. That's not about to change. I'm not going to be the one presiding over the meeting where nothing gets done."

Way to go, Josh! Not only had he put out the fire, but in the process he had recaptured his audience and reasserted his position.

"Well, since we've restored some order . . ." Brandon started to speak.

"Sit down, you fuckin' poser!" Josh barked.

Whoa!

Remember when I said Josh sometimes had "filter" issues?

All eyes penetrated Josh.

Just like he had messed up with his "I had dibs" comeback to me in the boys' room, Josh had messed up here, only this latter instance was exponentially worse. Visions of votes of no confidence and impeachment proceedings entered my head.

"Wow," Josh whispered. He sat down on the edge of Mr. Bitner's desk. He appeared as visibly shaken by his own words as everyone else. "Um, I don't know what to say."

Should I do something? Should I say something? That's my best friend.

I looked around the room. Leslie and Sam (yes, even Sam) had horrific expressions that contained glimpses of regret and pity. Even Mr. Bitner was looking up from his novel, something he hadn't done even when all hell had been breaking loose a short time ago.

"I tell you what," Josh spoke again, softly but steadily. He ran his hand through his hair and wiped the corners of his mouth with his Heat dress. He looked over to the windows. "Brandon, um, why don't you come up here? Say a few words?"

Brandon didn't react for what seemed like the longest moment, but it was probably only a second or two. Then he hopped off the windowsill and headed up. As he walked by Josh, he nodded at him, but Josh didn't look up. Josh simply went to Brandon's spot on the windowsill beside Leslie.

"Okay." Brandon clapped once. "Thanks for giving me this opportunity to speak." He sat down on the front of Mr. Bitner's desk and smiled appreciatively. "I, um, really wanted to address every-one today, but, um, I didn't think it would be under such com-bustible circumstances." He forced an uneasy laugh.

I shuddered. Sometimes it was uncanny how much he reminded me of his father, and considering how attracted I am to Brandon . . . okay, let's not go there right now.

"Let me start by saying I *am* committed to the GSA. I *do* want to be here. I am here on my own, on my own volition. I wouldn't be here otherwise. Honest."

He held up his hand like a Boy Scout. (I wondered if anyone else caught the irony.)

"I understand if you feel I need to prove myself. I'm not offended by that." He motioned toward the windows. "Now as Josh said earlier, the GSA requires its members to demonstrate their commitment through activism, and by activism Josh said that means giving of your time and putting in work."

Not only was Brandon sounding sincere, but he was alluding to Josh in the process. Way to go, pretty boy!

"So right now, if it's okay with Josh, Leslie, and everyone else, I'd like to bat leadoff. I'd like to be activist number one. This is such an incredible turnout, and I'm prepared—with your permission—to set the activist example."

Leslie nodded emphatically and motioned demonstratively for him to proceed.

"Cool." Brandon clapped again and rubbed his hands together like a dice player waiting on his lucky roll—just like Josh at the last GSA meeting. "Leslie, I'm going to need your ottoman." He pointed to the carton underneath her feet.

"Do you need help?" Leslie slid off the sill and reached down for the box.

"No, I'd like to handle this on my own."

Brandon picked up the carton and brought it back to Mr. Bitner's desk. He opened it up, pulled out a spiral-bound notebook, and held it up.

"I know I don't have enough of these for everyone, so I'm gonna ask that you share or look on with someone. I'll make more." Brandon distributed the notebooks by placing stacks on the desks in the front rows. "This is something I threw together. Most of the information in here I found on the net. I'll give you a few moments

Phil Bildner

to glance through it. I've also listed links and attached a bibliography at the back."

A copy reached my desk. I flipped through the pages.

You threw this together?

I was awestruck by what I was looking at. This wasn't something he had just thrown together. This was . . . this was amazing.

I flipped to a tabbed section titled "Climate and Atmosphere." The information was presented like a comprehensive weather report that addressed what it was like for gay, lesbian, bisexual, and transgender students in high school. The results of recent surveys were presented in bar graphs and pie charts.

I glanced at it only briefly, but I was floored by the few numbers I managed to read:

·97% of students in public high schools regularly hear homophobic remarks from their peers.

·The typical high school student hears antigay slurs over twenty-five times a day.

·Nearly one-third of students identifying themselves as gay, lesbian, or bisexual were threatened and/or injured with a weapon at school in the past year, compared to less than one-tenth of their heterosexual peers.

I flipped to another page.

·Lesbian and gay youths are two to six times more likely to attempt suicide than other youths.

·Lesbians and gays may account for 30% of all suicides among teens.

·A study found that within a recent twelve-month period, 29% of students who identified themselves as gay, lesbian, or bisexual had attempted suicide, compared to 7% of other students.

·A second survey of gay, lesbian, and bisexual individuals reported a 41% suicide-attempt rate. The average age at the first attempt was twelve, and nearly one-third of those who had attempted suicide had done so three or more times.

I turned to a third section titled "I Didn't Know I Was Positive," which contained the terrifying results of a survey (presented once again in tables and graphs) about gay men who are HIV positive.

•Three-quarters of young gay men with HIV in the U.S. are unaware they are carrying the virus.

  •Over 90% of black men who are positive don't know it.

  •Nearly 60% of those who tested positive for the HIV virus considered themselves to be at low risk for HIV infection, even though half of the individuals who had tested positive said they had had unprotected sex with one or more partners within the previous six months.

I stared up at Brandon. Brandon had done this? My Brandon? I was beyond speechless.

"I'm not going to read this to you." Brandon was sitting on Mr. Bitner's desk again. "You can do that on your own. But definitely take a look at some of the things in here. Some of the numbers are pretty eye-opening. I'm still struck by some of them."

Not only was I amazed and impressed, but I was also proud. Brandon had constructed this thirty-two-page masterpiece. What he had put together was truly the work of an activist.

"I know a lot of the data in here are scary and disheartening, but there's one thing I want to point out to you that's actually quite encouraging. Check out the pages that discuss the attitudes of parents." He held up the page. "Parents are finally waking up, and if you want to be an activist right now, get your parents to wake up too. Parents are changing. We have to keep that momentum."

Brandon had me hooked. I had to read about it *now*.

Phil Bildner

·86% of parents favored policies to protect gay, lesbian, bisexual, and transgender students from harassment and discrimination.

·80% favored sensitivity training for teachers to help them deal with antigay harassment of students.

·82% were bothered by gay kids being "abused" at schools.

·79% were bothered by gay kids being "isolated" by other students.

·51% of parents wanted "positive information" about gay people included in middle and high school English and social studies classes.

"Now I have something else," Brandon added.

More? I looked up from my reading. My mouth literally dropped.

Brandon trotted over to Leslie and Josh again, but this time he stopped before he reached them. He grabbed his JanSport off the floor and pulled out a large stack of papers.

"I know I have plenty of these." He placed half on a desk by the windows and jogged across the room to place the other half on a desk by the door. He held one up as they circulated. "These didn't cost nearly as much to make, and I used good old-fashioned staples." He thumbed through the five-page handout. "This handout is a little different from the one you just received. During my research, I came across a lot of firsthand accounts, anecdotes, and quotes, so I cut and pasted a bunch of them together. Some of them are funny, and some of them are absolutely tragic. They're about all different things: having a gay sibling, being gay and a minority, homophobia." He flipped to a page and pointed. "I really like the quotes from the different religious leaders. We hear so much about religion and homosexuality, and how the two concepts are inherently incompatible. It was refreshing to read writings and see excerpts from speeches given by respected religious leaders refuting that. What you hear at your place of worship, what you may be forced to listen to and even accept, may not be the universal belief."

I shook my head in disbelief.

"Now borrowing from another one of Josh's thoughts." Brandon nodded in Josh's direction again. "If you don't think you're going to read or use these materials, please don't take them. Leave them here. But if you want to read these or spread the word, then by all means do so."

I looked over at Leslie and Josh. Leslie was beaming like a proud parent, and Josh . . . Josh wasn't smiling, but he was looking through the materials. Yes, Brandon had managed to get Josh's attention.

"Okay, enough with the handouts," Brandon said, "let's get to the good stuff."

There was more?

Brandon leaned back and reached into the top drawer of Mr. Bitner's desk. He pulled out the remote for the two television monitors mounted from the ceiling at the front of the classroom. "Mr. B., does this have batteries?"

Even Mr. Bitner was paying attention now. He shook his head.

"That's okay. I brought extra just in case." Brandon pulled out a pair of AA batteries and put them in.

Brandon even thought of batteries! It was time to stop being amazed. It was time to simply appreciate and enjoy.

Brandon trotted over to the side of the room and flipped off the lights.

"The video's only about two or three minutes," Brandon explained. "I spliced together a series of PSAs—public service announcements—that focus on gay and lesbian youth. I downloaded them off the net. Some of you may have seen these on

Phil Bildner

MTV, CNN, E!, BET, or even during previews at the movies. I already synced up the monitors, so the clips should run simultaneously on both TVs.

Hold the phone!

Brandon knew he was going to do this all along. This was his I'm-gonna-take-care-of-it-don't-worry-about-it plan. Right down to the AA batteries and cueing up the DVD player in advance. Every last detail! This was *all* orchestrated!

This was all part of his silent treatment too. Sure the silent treatment was real, but at some point he had realized he was going to have to come around. Only he waited until this plan was in place. He *had* been listening to me all along. He knew he had to take Josh seriously. He just needed to do things *his* way. He couldn't ask me out—he wouldn't even talk to me—until his master plan was in order. (He probably didn't have the time either, considering the amount of work and effort he had put into this.)

I was so going to call him on all this when we went out this weekend. Definitely when we went out this weekend.

I glanced at Josh. His head was out of the handouts, and like everyone else he was staring intently at the television screens.

Even Sam had closed up her manicure shop and was watching.

"The first one is a series of 'snaps,'" Brandon said as the video started playing. "It's a montage of young people who have either experienced harassment, broken from traditional stereotypes, or are simply proud of their being."

I hadn't seen any of the PSAs contained in the montage, nor had I seen the full-length PSA of the mother reading excerpts from her teenage daughter's suicide note. I had seen the last one, which was of a high school kid walking through the hallway encountering an endless barrage of antigay abuse and harassment. In fact, I had seen that one with Josh during last year's Tonys or Oscars or Emmys — or whatever awards show it was that we absolutely couldn't miss.

When the videos ended — to another smattering of applause — Brandon flipped on the lights, but instead of returning to the front of the class, he ducked out into the hallway.

I peered over at Josh again. He still wasn't smiling, but he was certainly sitting up tall, and when Leslie leaned over and whispered something to him, he didn't bitch-slap her. Josh *had* to be feeling as warm and fuzzy as I was. He had feelings for Brandon just like I did (though only one of us was going to get to act on them).

Brandon reappeared in the doorway with yet another carton. This one was smaller, and once again he placed it on Mr. Bitner's desk.

"This is the last thing I have," Brandon said.

"That's it?" a joking voice called out. "You call this activism?"

The classroom laughed, including me, Sam, *and* Josh.

"Sorry, this is all I got." Brandon grinned. He opened the carton. "While putting together this presentation, I checked at the GSA office for resources. For those of you who don't know, the GSA office at Finley High consists of two bookshelves and an inbox outside Mr. Bitner's office next to the faculty lounge."

The classroom laughed again, including me, Sam, *and* Josh.

"One of the things I was looking for was information on Matthew Shepard, the college student who was murdered some years ago. In terms of mainstream America, this was the seminal event that really changed the way people viewed homophobia, hate crimes, and treatment of gays and lesbians." Brandon began removing items from the carton. "Unfortunately, I was surprised by the lack of resources. So while I was doing my research, every time I came across anything

Phil Bildner

related to the Matthew Shepard murder, I pulled it. That's what's here: articles, editorials, essays, interviews. I have copies of the TV movie based on him, as well as a DVD of *The Laramie Project*. I'm going to donate all this to the GSA, and hopefully now the GSA will merit its own bookcase or closet . . . that we all can come out of."

The classroom laughed again, including me, Sam, *and* Josh.

And that was it. That was how Brandon ended his perfect performance. He walked from the front of the room to thunderous applause and a standing ovation.

He walked straight over to me.

"Told ya not to worry 'bout it," he whispered in my ear. "Told ya I'd take care of things."

Yes, he had.

I looked over at Josh. He was standing by the windowsill in front of the very spot where Brandon now wanted to sit.

Josh looked at Brandon and nodded.

The nod.

That was it.

The nod. We were safe.

Brandon had saved my world, and he had saved the world as I knew it.

Josh headed back to the front of the room, but on his way he stopped dead in his tracks, pivoted, and walked over to me. He placed both hands on my desk and leaned in close. The look in his eyes confirmed everything.

"I'm in love," he whispered in my ear. "Brandon *has* to be gay. I love him now more than ever, Darcy."

That was going to be a problem. A big problem. But at this moment I didn't care. It didn't matter at all.

All that mattered was that Josh had called me Darcy.

I dropped my glove to the grass and knelt down to tie my already laced cleats.

Longdeeplongdeeplongdeep breath.

Walking out to the mound, I tingled all over. With every stride, I pounded my glove into my thigh like a jockey whipping a horse down the stretch. I needed to because I wasn't sure my wobbling legs would get me to my destination! Even when I toed the rubber and smoothed out the surrounding dirt—a little mound manicure, things need to be perfect—I was numb. My warm-up tosses helped cure my partial paralysis, but the jitters returned as soon as my catcher sent my final pitch, the ball customarily thrown down to second base, fifteen feet over Sam's and Brandon's heads into centerfield.

My phony shoelace job wasn't helping, so I stood back up. I tucked my glove under my arm, massaged the ball with both hands, and looked around. Maybe if I soaked in and savored the moment, my nerves would ease.

As for my teammates, Brandon and Sam stood behind second base with their gloves over their mouths deciding base coverages; my third baseman busily cleaned every last speck of dirt from his base (he's a tad anal); and out in left-center my outfield congregated for one last group chest-bump.

The Danforth Dragons sat on the bench behind third base. Moments from the opening pitch I expected to see their leadoff batter and *maybe* their on-deck batter sizing me up. Instead the scene resembled a zoo at feeding time. Every player was clinging to the protective fence and gawking at me. Coaches, too!

Over by home plate I was generating much the same reaction: Both umpires stood, mouths agape, with no-way-is-that-a-girl-throwing-warm-up-pitches-like-that expressions.

Both sets of bleachers behind the first- and third-base lines were packed like never before for a regular season game. In fact, the total number of people present easily exceeded the number of spectators who attended all of my girls' home softball games in my entire Finley career!

I searched for familiar faces. I spotted Samantha first. Of course I spotted Sam first. She was standing on the top row along the first base line, gabbing on her cell (shocking!) and waving to Sam at second. In Samantha's world, that's considered multitasking.

Josh was sitting a few rows in front and a few people over from Samantha. I'm sure they hadn't seen one another, because there's no way in hell they would have intentionally sat in such close proximity, and if either had spotted the other, they certainly would've relocated.

ICBM happened to be in the bleachers too. Talk about poetic justice! He was sitting with his fellow wannabes, and knowing ICBM, he was probably trying to convince them *he* played a role in my success.

Then I spotted them sitting in the bleachers behind third base. *Them.* Mom, Principal Basset, and Sequel.

I visibly gasped.

Nathalie Miller, I'm going to kill you! It wasn't enough that she had to be cozying up with the principal in front of the entire student body, but she had to bring the dog? Why didn't she just bring a personal spotlight? Bringing a dog to a high school sporting event is tantamount to driving a Hummer through an urban street fair. What was she thinking? Didn't she know that . . .

"Play ball!" the umpire shouted.

And if ever I needed a sentence to shout me back down to the land of the living, it was that eight-letter one.

This was it!

Showtime.

The leadoff batter for the Dragons liked to bunt, so I decided to start him off with a fastball in, and just as I expected, he squared around but he didn't offer. My pitch caught the inside corner for strike one.

I followed that up with a fastball away, which caught the outside corner for strike two. I didn't think either pitch had been a strike, but if Umpire Marlboro Man (that's what he looked like, so that's what I named him) was going to give me a generously wide strike zone, I wasn't about to complain.

With an 0–2 count, I wasted my next pitch. I doubted Leadoff Guy was going to chase a pitch a foot outside, but it was worth a shot. He didn't bite. Ball one.

I had thrown three fastballs, so I decided to see what Leadoff Guy could do with an inside changeup. Answer: Absolutely nothing.

Jammed!

Leadoff Guy tapped meekly to third for an easy five-three groundout.

The place erupted. My teammates stood on the bench and cheered. The fans in the bleachers "raised the roof." Irv and Bro bashed elbows. My catcher pumped both fists like he was posing in front of a weight-room mirror. The infield whipped the ball around.

All I could do was place my glove over my face and smile. It was a groundout for god's sake, not a game-winning grand slam!

I threw four straight off-speed pitches to Number Two Hitter, jammed him worse than Leadoff Guy, and retired him on a pop to third.

Two up, two gimmes to third, two down. This was too easy.

The Dragons' Three Batter was by far their best hitter, and as he stepped to the plate, he tried to intimidate me with a stare-down.

Puh-lease.

I knew he never swung at the first pitch, so I grooved a fastball right down the middle. I'm telling you, the only time you ever see a pitch that fat is in tee ball! I followed that up with a change, and Three Batter was so far out in front he finished swinging before the ball reached the plate. That drew some cackles from my infield, and it also started rhythmic clapping in the bleachers. The fans wanted a strikeout.

I had thrown ten pitches in the inning, all fastballs and change-ups. Now it was time for my curveball.

Yes, that's right. It was time for my curveball.

Despite *everyone* knowing my business, this was the one item I had managed to keep for myself. I had been practicing my curveball on my own. Without anyone knowing. For this very moment. *My* moment.

Not only *can* I throw a curveball, I'm *allowed* to throw a curveball. Situations don't dictate Darcy Miller. Darcy Miller dictates situations. Darcy Miller can take care of herself.

My catcher flashed the signs. I shook him off five straight times. He stood up, lifted his mask onto his head, and stared at me, puzzled.

I nodded at him knowingly, and that's when he figured out what

Phil Bildner

I wanted, what I *needed*. He squatted back down and dropped two fingers under his mitt. I smiled.

Showtime!

Can I tell you? I threw the nastiest hook that ever left my arm. I froze Three Batter like a Popsicle and caught him looking for strike three.

A one-two-three inning.

And I thought the place had erupted before? I was mobbed by every single member of the Finley baseball team.

But there was no time to bask and revel. I quickly found my batting gloves, helmet, and bat, and sized up a few warm-up tosses from the on-deck area. And waited. And waited.

This was it.

But no way was I taking a single step toward that batter's box without my proper introduction.

Until I heard those magic words. The words I needed. The only words I wanted to hear.

"Leading off: Darcy Miller."

About the Author

Phil Bildner

teaches middle-school history and English in the New York City public schools. He is the author of several picture books, including *The Shot Heard 'Round the World*; *Twenty-One Elephants*, recipient of the Oppenhiem Toy Portfolio Platinum Award; and the Texas Bluebonnet Award–winning *Shoeless Joe & Black Betsy*. This is his first novel.

Printed in the United States
By Bookmasters